BLIND LOVE
Like A Tiger

a novel by
D. James Benton

Synopsis

Quentin is awkward and very self-conscious about his appearance. Ann is breathtaking: beautiful, smart, funny, and completely blind. He can't verbalize his love for her but demonstrates it by delivering the ultimate gift: Ravi... After being attacked by a bat-wielding purse-snatcher, Ann is left without a guide dog and a six-month wait for a replacement. Quentin must act now! So he brings Ravi with assurances that Ann will never be accosted again. Quentin leaves several bags of Ravi's "special diet" and insists barking will not be a problem. The next morning Ann heads off to work in the City, scattering pedestrians along the way. For some reason, they won't let her on the bus. When Ann finally arrives at work, a coworker gasps, "That ain't no guide dog!" Ann counters sarcastically, "Cat's don't get this big." The coworker explains, "That kind do!" In that moment, Ann makes the connection and their lives change forever.

Table of Contents

Chapter 1. The Crisis

He gasped and collapsed onto the couch, heart racing, eyes bulging, and hands trembling. His mind struggled to comprehend the Reporter's voice, so focused was his attention on the limp figure being lifted on the stretcher into the ambulance. How could this be? Who would attack a blind girl? And for a second time! Would that it were *him* instead of her. Would that he had made good on his oath the *last* time. His own words, "Never Again," stampeded from the recesses of his consciousness like an approaching herd of buffalo, producing waves of sobbing. What could he possibly do? How could he have prevented this? If he had been by her side, what chance would he have against a bat-wielding purse-snatcher? His physique couldn't intimidate a squirrel. In his mind, he took on the form of a squirrel, cowering in fear before some predator. In that moment it hit him—the solution—the ultimate protection for the love of his life: Ravi!

Earlier that Evening

Quentin Farley switched on the evening news in hopes of hearing that the players and owners had reached some agreement and the all-important sport of hockey could resume. "Why can't they settle this on the ice?" he inquired aloud to the four walls of his tiny apartment in Queens. Video snippets from various camera angles around the subway played as some reporter rambled on about the deplorable lawlessness beneath the streets of New York City. "Another woman has fallen victim to the snatch-and-shove bandit."

Quentin went to the fridge in search of a beer. As he slid out the drawer and reached for the bottle opener, the Reporter explained, "This latest victim has been attacked before."

He applied the opener, stepped on the pedal of the trashcan, and disposed of the cap in a single well-practiced motion. Video of a person on a stretcher being wheeled away from the train platform played as Quentin approached the television, mildly interested.

An emergency medical technician and uniformed police officer kneeling beside a lifeless German shepherd wearing some kind of harness filled the screen, as the Reporter continued, "Not only was this latest victim blind, but the attacker beat her dog to death." Quentin clutched the beer, as realization swept over him.

The scene changed to show a different reporter holding a microphone up to the face of the woman on the stretcher, who wept piteously. "He died protecting me. Toby was more than a guide. He was my friend."

1

The blind woman attacked in the subway was Ann Draper! The bottle slipped from Quentin's hand and fell to the floor, as he sank onto the couch. This couldn't be happening... not again! Not to Ann. The one for whom his heart beat. The one who held his heart in her hands. The one for whom he would gladly die—if only he could take her place.

Where It All Started

That day six long years ago changed his life. Being a new kid in a new school with no friends is bad enough, but when you're a nerd's nerd on steroids and look exactly like one of the characters in the latest video game, it's a double nightmare. That the anime character is named Quint and is also a total loser doesn't help either.

Quentin plopped down in the nearest available desk and began rummaging through his backpack. He didn't notice that several students were stifling chuckles at his expense. That's when *it* happened. A girl *sat* on him, fell over backwards, somehow got a strap around his neck, which was connected to a dog, which barked and tugged, having the result that they all—him, the girl, his backpack, her backpack, and the desk, toppled over with the dog dragging the entire mess out into the hallway. It didn't help that he elbowed her and blurted, "Klutz!" This he did before noticing that she was positively breathtaking—beautiful beyond description.

Time stopped, the heavens opened, and angelic voices began singing some unknown chorus, as the two struggled to disentangle themselves and stand. He still hadn't figured out yet—even with the strange harness and dog—that the girl was blind. It wasn't until he braced himself, stood up, and broke the oddly familiar red-striped white stick that she had dropped, that a neuron deep in some little-used node of his brain flashed: she's *blind*!

Quentin's mind began to race, spewing forth every form of apology residing within his gray matter. What came out of his mouth was like the sounds in the night that awaken hung-over graduate students assigned to the search for extraterrestrial intelligence who are being pranked. By contrast, she was most gracious, especially considering the flummox he had brought upon her.

"I'm so sorry," she apologized. "This is my assigned seat. It's right by the door. I should have tapped first." As she explained, she felt for the stick and then realized what the cracking sound meant. The disappointment on her face was clearly evident.

At this moment, the Teacher strode into the room and looked down upon them with annoyance... well, mostly at him. The dog tilted its head as if to say, "Don't look at me. This was all Stupid's fault."

Quentin held up the broken end of the stick and mumbled, "Maybe we can glue it back together."

2

The Teacher took both pieces, walked to the desk, pulled out the lower drawer, and joined the parts together with some sturdy-looking tape. She then returned and placed the top end of the stick into the girl's hand and folded her fingers around it. This seemed to help the situation considerably, at least from the expression on the girl's face, who said, "I'm Ann," and extended her other hand.

He gingerly took her hand and stammered, "Quentin."

As the three righted the desk and restored order, he noticed there were snickers and chuckles about the classroom. The dog was remarkably calm and seemed almost bored with the situation. Ann took her proper place in the desk and the dog promptly sat beside her. Quentin plopped into a desk at the back of the room, wishing he could shrivel up and die. The Teacher looked about and announced, "Now that the Battle of the Desk is over, we will consider the Battle of the Bulge, one of the most decisive moments in World War Two."

* * *

To say their first meeting had been less than idyllic would be the greatest understatement of all time. To say that it had little impact on him would be even more inaccurate. Quentin's obsession with Ann grew by the day, as did his self-flagellation over making such a mess of things. He had for years joked with a few friends—all left behind at the previous school—that only a blind girl would ever fall for him. Well... she had literally fallen on him and was literally blind. Was there a chance of her falling for him? About like that proverbial snowball in the fires of perdition.

Still, he dreamed of her day and night. Every time their paths crossed, he was exceedingly careful—and quiet too. It was some time in the second week after their first oops that he noticed that she turned her head, positioning her ear toward him. On the following day she said, "You don't have to tippy-toe around. I'm not going to sit on you again."

What? How? Had the dog alerted her some way to his presence? Was she not totally blind? "So sorry," he whimpered. "I didn't want to startle you." At this point he could swear the dog was grinning and in on the joke.

"It's OK," she explained. "I don't easily startle. It does help me navigate when people make some noise, so scuff your feet maybe."

He looked down and wiggled one foot, which didn't make what one might call a scuffle—not surprising for sneakers.

"I'm just kidding," she soothed. "You could whistle a tune or pretend to argue with Abraham Lincoln or Thomas Jefferson."

Her demeanor quickly lifted him from the doldrums of self-doubt. As they proceeded to the next class he suggested, "I could pretend to have an emotional support cat—one that likes dogs, of course." He said, "meow," the dog let out a little, "woof," and they both laughed. It was their first *real* conversation and it

3

went very well. He couldn't tell you a single thing that happened for the rest of the day if his life depended on it. The last thing he did remember from that day was drifting off to sleep, dreaming of the two of them running through the heather, swinging a picnic basket on a perfect day with the guide dog and emotional support cat bounding along beside them.

Chapter 2. The Solution

Quentin stood on the doorstep trembling with apprehension. Would this extravagant gift make or break the relationship? Did they even have a relationship? Would it convey his desperate love or breathtaking stupidity? The tiger looked sympathetically up at his trainer, able to sense the anxiety even without the genetically enhanced cerebral cortex. So much effort... so much riding on this moment... so much to gain... so much to lose.

At last he reached out and pressed the buzzer, then held his breath, heart pounding, seconds passing. After what seemed like hours, Ann opened the door and said, "Hello. Who is it?"

"It's Qu... Quen, Nobody" he stammered, "with your replacement, Ravi."

"So soon!" Ann exclaimed. "Ever-Guard told me on the phone that I might have to wait six months."

"This is... um... different... uh... special..." Quentin mumbled, "because you're so very special... I mean your situation is special... and so is Ravi. He's extremely special. One of a kind, in fact! Well, two of a kind, really. He has a twin. If he works out with you, then Darcy will get Tavi, Ravi's twin."

The expression on Ann's face changed and his panic increased so that he quickly backtracked. "Oh, Ravi *will* work out OK. I promise! He's absolutely amazing. He's so smart he can fetch specific items: phone, slippers, even beer from the fridge." This had to work. If this didn't work, he might as well sit in the subway and wait for the Grim Reaper.

"Quentin..." she questioned. "Is that you?"

"Ye... yes," he stammered.

Is this possible? She recognized his voice? She remembered his name? She knew he existed? Is this a dream?

"Well, come in. Let's get acquainted."

"I'm Quentin Farley and this is Ravi Tig... Just Ravi."

"I know who you are, Quentin. I meant me and Ravi."

Ann walked over to the couch and sat. Ravi knew just what to do. He sat beside her and put his head in her lap. "Ooo... you are a big boy!" Ann cooed. "And so soft too. Are you going to protect me from the bad guys?"

Quentin sat down on the sectional opposite and remarked, "Trust me. You will never be accosted again." Then quickly added, "He has a very keen sense of danger."

5

Ann continued to explore with her hand, scratching and stroking. "Your fur is just wonderful! You aren't going to shed all over the place, I hope."

"No, no shedding. He's been staying with me and no fur problems." Ravi was clearly enjoying the meet-and-greet.

"Please don't growl or make any tiger noises," Quentin prayed.

"I hope he doesn't bark a lot. My landlord is such a grouch. He can hear a cat meow at a thousand yards in a gale."

"He'll wet his pants when this cat meows," Quentin thought but said, "Trust me. Barking won't be a problem. Not once. Never heard a bark."

Stop over-stating it. Just give the simple facts and leave it there.

"I bet you eat a lot," Ann said wryly.

"That reminds me," Quentin interjected. "He's on a special diet. I brought some bags and can bring more. I'll just go out to the car and get them."

When he returned with the bags, Ann was shaking Ravi's paw. "Ooo... what big paws you have!"

Please don't say, "What big teeth you have!"

"He knows to wipe his feet before coming in," Quentin added hopefully. "Your eye still looks pretty bad. How's the shoulder?" he asked, changing the subject.

"The swelling has gone down a lot and it doesn't hurt as bad," she replied. "I've got a couple more weeks in the sling."

"It is so disgusting that some creep would snatch a purse—from a blind person, no less. Then shove you down plus whack your dog!"

"Toby went for him even before I could feel the tug on my purse strap. Dogs have a sense about danger and he could tell the guy was up to no good. Toby gave his life to save me from getting bonked on the head. I miss him so much. He was so much more than a guide. He was a friend. I don't know if I will ever bond with another. I couldn't bear having another friend ripped away so horribly."

After a minute-long pause Quentin spoke. "Ravi also has a good sense of danger and will protect you to the uttermost. He is loyal and I hope you will one day be as close to him as you were to Toby."

"I had several police officers apologize to me at the scene and later at the hospital. They try to make the streets and subway safe but it's an overwhelming job. There are so many bad guys and so few of them. I have heard them say that you can't just look at someone and tell if they're a criminal or not. Just because some guy wears a hoodie in the middle of the summer and shuffles along looking at the ground with hands in pockets doesn't mean they're about to snatch a purse or rob a liquor store."

6

"I guess not. If you watch the news, you'd think the cops base everything on stereotypes but I guess that's just an over-generalization by people who would hate the cops, whatever they did or didn't do."

"At least the guy didn't have a gun—or if he did, didn't use it on me or Toby. I think I'd wet myself if someone fired a gun near or at me."

"Ravi's pretty tough and astonishingly fast," Quentin said reassuringly. "If someone pulls a gun on you, they'll be dead before they can squeeze the trigger."

"He's not one of those pit bulls," Ann inquired tentatively. "I guess they have short hair."

"No, nothing like a put bull. Just a big cuddly ball of fur with really sharp tee—toes, I mean toes... paws... feet! Really big feet. That's it. Really big feet. He will stomp any purse-snatcher."

Please don't ask what breed he is!

Quick, change the subject!

"It must be difficult having your purse snatched," Quentin asked nervously.

"At least I don't carry anything of value," Ann sighed. "I do have a credit card but it has a $500 limit and it's up to about $450 at the moment. The worst is that they took my phone. To get that replaced and switched over means two bus rides plus the subway plus nineteen blocks on foot. I can never remember all the twists and turns. By the time I get there, I'm hoarse from asking directions."

"Wow! I hadn't thought about that. I've only been to the phone store once. Since then everything has been through the mail with no real urgency."

"Thankfully, I had my swipe card for the Station on a lanyard and so they didn't get that."

"I just love your show and listen to the Station whenever I can," Quentin interjected.

"It really is my dream job," Ann explained. "I love hearing and sharing stories, interacting with people, and listening to the music. It's still a little hard to believe they pay me to do it."

"Beats working at the DMV or flipping burgers plus you never have to ask, "Do you want fries with that?"

The two laughed and Quentin relaxed just a little.

Wrap this thing up before she asks any questions about Ravi.

"Of course, Ravi is house-broken," Quentin added. "He does this thing with his paw and you just have to open the door."

"Great. I'll let him out back in the rear courtyard. My Dad comes over on Sunday afternoon and does poop patrol."

The rest of their conversation went well and the word, "tiger," was never mentioned. Quentin slipped out to the car and slumped over the wheel, exhausted from the anxiety.

Chapter 3. The Lecture

Quentin Farley was truly extraordinary in many ways, including intellect. Some teachers appreciated this, while others couldn't get past his awkwardness and strange behaviors. He excelled scholastically so that he earned a two-year degree and was half way through the junior year in college soon after he finished high school. Before he finished the senior year, he had started on graduate courses. Quentin's passion was genetics but his heart was ever pulled toward habitat—that is, the harmful effects of chemicals on the environment and wildlife. He had a genuine passion to save the Planet.

Above all, Quentin was focused; yet, he seemed to have one foot on the dock and the other on a boat with the two drifting apart. A professor insisted, "You must choose a single area of focus: genetics or the environment. You can't do both. That's just the way it is." And so he stumbled along, taking the courses that most interested him, ignoring whether or not these were moving toward completing any particular course of study.

Weeks turned into months, which turned into semesters. There was more than enough to fulfill his thirst for knowledge and so far, nobody had raised the specter of the scholarship running out. His grandparents had set aside a trust for him and the three other cousins, which was adequate for everything else. He was driving Grammy's old Taurus, after they took her keys away. She was in a nursing home now. The car was old and a bit of a gas-guzzler, but it ran and that was enough.

The University was always hosting conferences, some of which were worth his time and effort to get in without paying the absurd registration fees. A few of the speakers were interesting, but none really struck a resonant chord with his passions. Near the end of that semester came a big conference with many top-notch speakers, called TOOT. There were so many jokes floating about the acronym that no one seemed to know what it really stood for.

In spite of the jokes, TOOT held some promise and so Quentin secured a free pass, complete with nametag, after making a passionate appeal to some officious-looking person in the Graduate School, which was housed in a building he visited as infrequently as possible. Quentin still had not gotten a satisfactory answer as to why, if they have no faculty and offer no classes, does the Graduate School bestow degrees. Why not the various Departments or Colleges?

At last, TOOT arrived. This opportunity came with more decisions: which lecture to attend when two essential ones were running simultaneously? One lecture fairly leapt off the brochure and slapped him across the face: Genetic Impacts of Micro-Pollutants. Quentin soaked up every word and slide in the presentation. One comment in particular piqued his interest... "The vast majority of these chemicals that can cause even minute changes in DNA have devastating impacts," the speaker sighed deeply before continuing. "Strangely enough, there is one, cyclo-dec-la-mide, that may possibly enable us to fix some of that. It's still a long shot but we would be glad to have anything in our tool bag."

When the presentation ended, Quentin dashed to engage the speaker, Dr. Peter Booth, and hear more. "Tell me more about this cyclodeclamide!"

"Well, we're not quite sure but it may splice a fragment from the end of one DNA chain onto another. We first noticed this when mu-cela-did-ae showed up in storm water at Percy Air Force Base where only bar-ga-nelle had been a problem," Booth explained.

"How did you come to that conclusion?" Quentin inquired, interested but somewhat skeptical.

"It's a clean-up operation. They have some really nasty stuff—don't ask where it came from but *we* didn't make it. Our Team is very careful that none of it gets into the environment. One of the nasties is barganelle, which is chlorine resistant. Muceladidae is not—like most organisms—and not a problem; or at least wasn't until something happened and it became chlorine resistant. Only at this site—don't ask how many sites there are—like I said, we didn't create this mess. We just clean it up."

Quentin was completely engaged by this point and Booth could sense it—a sincerely interested student with a passion for the environment. This was a nice change from the usual, "Just clean it up—thoroughly, of course—and let me know when it's done." That he so often got. Booth elucidated, "The chlorine resistance only presented itself at Percy. The only difference I could find was the cyclodeclamide, which is from another project—don't ask. Just because I'm a tiny bit OCD, I created a controlled experiment with the two species and one agent. Shazam! Chlorine resistance. I tried the same thing with a different species, pro-ci-len-na, and squat! Yes and No are both important answers in this business."

Quentin and Peter could be cousins as far as mannerisms, brilliance, and interests. A student-teacher bond was quickly forming and so the student exclaimed, "And if cyclodeclamide can do that... then what else can it do?"

"Precisely!" Booth declared. "We may finally be able to fix genetic defects in endangered species!"

"Oh, that I could be involved with that effort!" Quentin sighed.

"Maybe you can. There is more than enough work and thankfully adequate funding. We can always use another hand and a fresh perspective. It helps when you've been staring through a microscope at the same thing for months on end to

10

get new eyes on it. There is a lot of boring and tedious work but even that has its benefits if you let it."

"Oh, I'm good with boring and tedious, especially if there's even a glimmer of light at the end of the tunnel."

"I have a brief meeting and then we break for lunch. Are you up for the Falafel Hut if I'm buying?"

"I'm always up for the Falafel Hut!"

"Then I'll see you there at half past."

* * *

They got their orders and sat at a table, where Booth spread out a series of documents related to the clean-up operation and the side interest of gene splicing. These would make little sense to most, but Quentin dove right in, absorbing the diverse information. These included gene sequencing maps, which Quentin had seen but never created himself—a skill he hoped to acquire.

"Just ignore the names," Booth explained. "It's best to ask as few questions as possible so that if anyone ever drags you into a little room with an uncomfortable chair and bright lights you can honestly say you're clueless."

"Oh, I'm pretty good at clueless," Quentin chuckled.

"Some of these things sound like an apocalyptic movie where a rabid bat bites a guy working at a bio weapons lab and then bites another guy who sells dim sum from a push cart in Kao Loon. Then it quickly spreads around the world, killing everyone who doesn't have Rh-null blood type *and* a life-threatening peanut allergy."

"I think I saw that one on Netflix at least twice."

"The folks at the Pentagon are running three ways from Sunday, stamping out fires all over the world that never make it into the news. This isn't their only crisis and they don't give it their undivided attention. Still, I can tell that they—at least the ones I deal with—really do care and will see it through to the end, whatever it takes," Booth explained. "So I leave it at that and do the best I can. Same goes for the rest of the Team. I don't ask, 'Why?' or ,'Who?'. I just ask, 'What do you need me to do next?'"

This description of environmental clean-up wasn't anything like Quentin had imagined or how it was portrayed in the news, but he could work with it. Doing the best you can with what you have to work with is a lot better than pointing fingers and directing blame and fussing while doing nothing as bloated whales float up on the beach.

"There are no atta-boys in this job and no celebrity award banquets but you can put your head down on the pillow at night knowing the world is a little bit better off today than it was yesterday because of something you did," Booth concluded.

11

"That's enough for me," Quentin added. "I'm not into all the fuss anyway."

Chapter 4. The Project

Quentin's studies continued, with lectures, labs, homework, and tests, but no progress on narrowing down the focus of his graduate studies. The department was settled but the topic and advisor wasn't. One day as Quentin and five other students were analyzing a sample of water from a nearby lake, Dr. Booth appeared at the door of the laboratory. Quentin excused himself and withdrew to the hallway. Booth wore a smile that bode of adventure. "I have a proposition for you if you're interested and can keep a few secrets—all in the interest of national security, of course. Perfectly legitimate."

"Sounds wonderful!"

"As we discussed, it would be my life's dream to *repair* damaged DNA in an endangered species. I think your dream too."

Quentin nodded enthusiastically and Booth continued, "We would have to *prove* the method first, as the risk is much too great otherwise."

"Yes, of course!"

"We must select a useful test case. If it works, we go up a notch. If that works, we go up another notch. Who knows how long it will take or if we can ever make it work but it's worth a try, right?"

"Oh, yes, we must try!"

"It's going to cost a fortune." Quentin's countenance fell. "But the Pentagon has plenty of money."

"Why would they fund such an effort?" Quentin inquired.

"Oh, they'll fund anything if it fits into their bigger plan," Booth reassured.

"Are they interested in endangered species?"

"Not specifically, but there is a huge push right now to incorporate more support animals."

"Like to find bodies and sniff out bombs?"

"Exactly, plus other types of danger that animals seem to be more aware of than people. Cows lie down before it snows. They're more accurate than the Weather Channel."

"And humming birds fly back to the same city in Mexico each year when the weather is just right for their migration," Quentin added with delight.

"Birds begin gobbling up seeds days before any meteorologist knows the weather is changing."

"What if we can isolate that part of their DNA and use cyclodeclamide to splice it into a dog's."

"Voilà! Rover the weather pooch is born!"

"That would be a dream come true."

"Of course, we may not find the weather gene right off and we may not be able to splice it into dog DNA but we can find something and hopefully splice it somewhere and make some progress."

"Let's do it!" Quentin said triumphantly, then sighed. "But I still have to figure out something here at school."

"I'm an adjunct professor on staff here," Dr. Booth explained. "I can be your advisor and sell the rest on the idea."

"That would be awesome!"

"No one else here needs to know the why or the who, how we decide or where we get the stuff to work on. Instead of the funds coming from the Department of Defense, which can be problematic, they will come from CleanWater, Inc., who gets them from the DoD."

"Works for me."

"You can come up with a goal and title for your thesis that is achievable. Don't promise to colonize Jupiter. If we get there, great, but you don't want your success here to rest on that."

"How about Gene Splicing in Single-Cell Aquatic Organisms?"

"That would raise too many eyebrows," Booth suspected. "How about Circumventing Chlorine Resistance in Single-Cell Aquatic Organisms?"

"I like that one. It sounds like we're eliminating some nasties, which I'm sure we can find a way to accomplish," Quentin suggested.

"Oh, yeah, even a little bit of ozone will knock them right out. It's more expensive and more hassle to work with, but it gets the job done."

* * *

They filled out the necessary forms and met with several of the other faculty. Then Quentin made a presentation and the thesis proposal was accepted. Quentin was assigned a dingy little laboratory, which also served as a makeshift office. Dr. Booth got to put an old desk and empty filing cabinet in a supply closet at the farthest end of the hall, away from the departmental office, copier, mailboxes, and meeting room. He dutifully showed up every Monday afternoon from one to five, attended as few meetings as possible, and stayed out of the turf wars, which dwarfed the great battles over the literal Holy Land. He had enough of that garbage during his own university ordeal. This effective isolation facilitated productivity and suited the temperament of student and professor, alike as they were.

14

* * *

The quantitative groundwork had to come first. Up until this time, the primary concern had been bringing the nasties down to the non-detect level, which was defined by EPA standards. This was a go-no-go sort of evaluation and not a quantitative one—good enough for fieldwork but not for the laboratory and university-level research. Quentin had to analyze hundreds of samples, which meant being hunched over a microscope for as long each day as he could bear. Then there were the metabolic tests—kind of like checking to see if the tuna salad that's been in the fridge for a month has turned blue and grown a beard. One series of tests with chlorine, one with bromine, and one with ozone, just to cover all the bases. The details were filling multiple spreadsheets and more than a few graphs, which would eventually make it into the Thesis.

Quentin's laboratory/office was always quiet—except when there was some outside source of noise. The department building was positioned near the Stadium so that whenever there was a home game or concert or other event, he could not stand to be there. During those times he would often walk one of the many nature trails in the area. His favorite one was a tree-lined winding path that followed the outline of a pond. Birds, squirrels, and an occasional rabbit would entertain him on the walk. These were times of rest and recovery.

In the evenings, Quentin alternated between binge watching television series, reading historical novels—the factual, not the mushy kind, and listening to WNYG, which billed itself as, 'Totally Uplifting Radio'. This same radio station was the workplace of the love of his life, Ann. The music was great and they did mention her occasionally, but Ann was only on air in the afternoons. He would wait for her to come on the air before breaking to eat his lunch. He would ration this time out so as to not seriously diminish his laboratory time. When it didn't bring his lunch, there was a sandwich shop just three blocks away that played WNYG constantly.

Quentin often felt like he was living someone else's life or was stuck inside someone else's body. Whatever, it wasn't working out. In some ways—scholastically—he was advancing through time, but in other ways—emotionally, where it counts—he was frozen in time and stuck in high school. Ann was everything he wanted in life but they had hardly spoken in the year they attended the same school.

Quentin's father worked for a wholesale office supply company that sold a variety of items to schools and businesses. The Farley family lived in a suburb of Asheville, North Carolina that had a small-town look and feel. Near the end of Quentin's junior year of high school, a promotion came through that meant moving to New York City and came with a significant raise. While Quentin's father had traveled to the Big Apple many times, moving there was culture shock for Quentin and his mother.

Not only would starting as a senior in a new city at a new school be difficult for any student, this was particularly difficult for Quentin, for he was very awkward physically and behaviorally. His nose was much too big and chin much too small and ears much too flappy not to draw ridicule from other students who delight in causing such misery. One thing that did work to slightly reduce the teasing was that Quentin was uncommonly smart. This meant that he took advanced classes where available. The students most prone to bullying were often stuck in remedial classes.

Ann was smart too and so their classes overlapped. After she sat on him one day, their awkward and mostly silent relationship began. He was always super careful not to bump into her again—in the literal sense, which minimized the opportunities to talk. He just couldn't bring himself to literally bump into her just to start a conversation and he was too shy to start one otherwise.

Chapter 5. The Embryos

After nearly two years and countless hours in the laboratory nurturing slime, ooze, and a variety of insects, Quentin defended his thesis and was awarded a master's degree. The funding—it wasn't all that much—continued to trickle in. The following door was open: doctoral research. This was the next "notch" Quentin and Peter had discussed so many times. It took surprisingly little effort to sell the faculty on the plan, but a surprising number of forms to fill out and fees to pay to get the Graduate School—whatever the heck they have to do with this process is still a deeply shrouded mystery to all but a select few— rolling with the flow. The *important* part of the Plan was, of course, discussed over lamb gyros at the Falafel Hut.

"It's got to be mice or rabbits," Booth insisted.

"I just can't bear the thought of hurting them."

"Rats then. Nobody likes rats."

"But I do..."

"We'll get them from the sewer or the dump. The Lab will be a step up for them."

"It's the same thing either way. I just can't do it."

"We've got to step up to mammals if we're ever going to get where we ultimately want to be."

"OK then, but what about the donor species?"

"Pigeons. Nobody likes pigeons."

"But I do..."

"Then use your own DNA," Booth suggested, but only as a joke.

"OK. I'll do it," Quentin said with finality, chomping down on the gyro with determination. "I will splice my DNA onto sewer rats."

"At least it's not NIMH or we'd be in big trouble."

"NIMH?"

"You know, the story about Mrs. Frisby and the Rats of NIMH that are super intelligent and escape. I have read it to my niece and nephew a hundred time. They just love it."

"Then we can't do it. We can't have rats with my DNA escaping and destroying the environment."

"Read them the story and explain how this is their great contribution."

17

"Seriously?" Quentin balked. "And they're just going to bow to the greater good and agree to live in a cage?"

"If they're smart enough to understand the story you can take them home and they can live with you. Besides, if they have any of your DNA they'll probably embark on a crusade to clean up the sewers."

"OK, let's get started."

"Don't forget to fill out the paperwork. They're fussy about that stuff."

"Tell me again what the Graduate School contributes to this process?" Quentin inquired.

"Absolutely nothing," Booth replied. "In the positive sense, of course. They do introduce you to filling out useless and utterly stupid paperwork, which is important preparation for most jobs, especially working with the Pentagon."

"Plus they introduce you to a mind-boggling hierarchy of redundant bureaucrats whose entire existence is to justify their entire existence."

* * *

The experiments began and the funding increased. Nothing seemed to change. Nobody at the University seemed to notice or care what was going on in the Laboratory in the basement at the dark end of the hall where the nameless machines whirred and the pipes gurgled endlessly. Sadly, the first two generations of rats didn't live long. These weren't actually real sewer rats, just some from a pet store. Quentin and Peter decided to coax Peter's brother-in-law, who was outdoorsy, to trap some real sewer rats. "Make it sound like a big game hunt and he'll come through for us." These did rather well but nothing happened—at least not that either of the scientists could detect. Still, they were much cuter than Quentin expected and soon became pets.

After nine months of experiments, it seemed that one generation of rats had "inherited" the human couch potato gene, thanks to cyclodeclamide, as all they did was eat and sleep. Quentin set up a television for them but they showed little interest in it. They could, however, detect food wrapped in plastic, or so it seemed, as they would perk up before Quentin stepped into the room.

He set up a camera and was astonished to see them stir when he was half way down the hall. This wasn't the desired objective, but it did provide some encouragement. Rats that can detect food from a mile away, devour an astonishing amount, and sleep on the couch are not exactly the sort of achievement to earn a Nobel Prize, more like free meals and a bed in a 6-by-6 cell. Quentin worried and wondered if you had to get approval to do such experiments and from who. "Perhaps fill out a form and submit it to the Graduate School," he laughed aloud, then pushed these thought aside.

After Gen-CP, the couch potato generation, he began changing up the conditions when snipping off part of his DNA. This, finally, produced some more interesting results. Was it just his imagination or were these rats fascinated by nature shows on TV? Switch to Wheel of Fortune and they sulked off to the activity wheel for some exercise. Seriously? Even rats won't watch Wheel of Fortune? Not sure how or if to work this one into the Dissertation.

These latest he designated Gen-TV. They also seemed to appreciate leftovers and were slightly picky concerning food—completely opposite of Gen-CP, which would gobble up anything from the trash. Quentin had been reluctant up until this point to assign names, rather using numbers. Gen-TV, however, consisted of Mrs. Frisby, of course, Jonathan, Martin, and Timothy. He even put a little cardboard sign on the corner of the cage that said, 'NIMH'. He didn't read them the story but did find the movie on Netflix, which Gen-TV watched with some interest. Gen-CP snored through the whole thing.

* * *

One day Booth appeared, breathless and bursting with excitement, having run from the car through the building and down the stairs, not waiting for the elevator. "It's happened! This is our big break. The opportunity we've waited for."

"Yes, I'm waiting with baited breath—whatever that means," Quentin exclaimed.

"Two tiger embryos from the National Zoo!"

"Why would they let us have them?"

"There was only one. It must have split. Identical twins maybe? They aren't sure. There may have been something wrong with the cryo-fridge so that everything thawed and refroze. The process is so expensive that they aren't willing to invest the money or effort to take it any farther. They were going to just toss them out but my sister works for the fridge company and said she'd try to do something. She contacted a big cat rescue place in North Carolina but they weren't interested. Then she called a dozen veterinaries and shelters. The ones that would discuss it wanted money. She told me and I said, 'We got the money and would love to have them!'"

"Let's do this thing!" Quentin pumped the air with expectation. "But wait... Where are we going to get a mama tiger to hatch them if the Zoo isn't interested?"

"It doesn't have to be a tiger. My golden retriever, Auro, is an excellent mother, will nurture them, and prepare them for a life of service."

"Forecasting the weather perhaps?"

"Who knows..."

"This latest batch, Gen-TV, could rate shows and even comment on the cooking channel, not that anyone would listen to the opinion of rats, of course."

19

"That you've been able to transfer anything that isn't lethal is remarkable progress. Let's just hope that the tigers don't end up on the cooking channel, extolling their recipes for Leg of Lucy and Adam's Ribs."

Chapter 6. The Bump

"You did *what*?!" the General roared. Dr. Booth feared the entire Pentagon was now on high alert. "We funded genetically-modified tigers? Are you insane? Have you sucked us into a horror film? How many people have they eaten?"

"They're absolutely adorable," Booth said reassuringly. "They're cuddly and incredibly smart. They can bring you a beer from the fridge. They can even count and distinguish colors—something dogs can't do."

"But genetically-modified? The animal rights people will burn us at the stake if word of this gets out!"

"They could be the ultimate protection for our people in the jungle or wherever, not just cadaver or bomb-sniffing, but *real* protection."

The General was sputtering and Booth was trembling. Quentin would be trembling too, if he were here, the two shared such behaviors. A colonel stuck her head into the room and made a little noise. "Sorry to interrupt, Sir, but I couldn't help but hear your discussion and might have a solution to your predicament."

"Please! Anything to clean up this disaster," the General pleaded.

"The ultimate protection, you say? Incredibly smart, you say? And cuddly to boot?" the Colonel reiterated with a wry smile.

"Yes, all those things and more," Booth replied.

"You know who needs that and could easily smooth out any bumps in the road with her irresistible charisma?" she inquired.

"Barnum & Bailey's Circus?" the General balked. "I think they're gone."

"Darcy Bates," the Colonel said with flourish.

"Who?"

"The President's blind daughter, who could charm monkeys out of the trees to offer their bananas."

"Doesn't she already have the Secret Service hanging about?"

"Yes, but she hates all the fuss and is always sneaking off."

"Even if she goes for it, the Secret Service never would."

"We just need to prove the concept and run it by her. She's been on that nature show talking about how a blind person is more in tune with the sounds of nature, especially birds."

"What do birds have to do with it?" the General objected.

"They're always talking about endangered species on that show and if the Professor explains how this experiment with the tigers was part of a bigger plan to possibly repair damaged DNA, she would be totally onboard."

"OK," the General conceded. "Let's get one of our service dog people involved and get these tigers—I can't believe I'm saying this—checked out and then run it by her and the Secret Service."

"I will see to it personally, Sir," the Colonel said, as she nodded to Booth.

* * *

Three weeks later, the Colonel, Dr. Booth, Quentin, and Tavi slipped into the Whitehouse at one in the morning under the cloak of darkness. Darcy and Tavi hit it off immediately. The three Secret Service wet blankets were not impressed—horrified, more like it. On command, Tavi fetched Darcy's phone and then the TV remote. The Three were slightly impressed and a little less horrified. Quentin put out four slippers: one each red, pink, yellow, and white. Tavi fetched the slippers, as selected by the Skeptical Service Agents in turn by color. They eased up a bit more. A half hour later they agreed that, after sufficient experience with another blind subject—not the President's daughter— they might accept Tavi on a trial basis, but would keep one hand on a gun at all times.

Darcy was ecstatic. Booth explained the bigger picture, emphasizing how very careful they were not to let anything out that wasn't thoroughly tested. He paused and Darcy interjected, "We don't want a repeat of Mrs. Frisby and the Rats of NIMH." Only one of the Secret Service agents laughed, recognizing the story reference. The others looked bored and ready to be done with these late night "guests".

* * *

As the Colonel, Booth, and Quentin were driving back from Washington, the mood in the car was mixed. The future was still a little murky. After a while, the Colonel said, "Don't worry. We'll find some blind person who will help us take the next step..."

"For now they need to keep a lid on the genetic modification part," Booth cautioned. "There will definitely be a backlash at some point over that. Let's hope we have some real progress to show by then."

"Tavi and Ravi are smarter than most of the politicians here," Quentin interjected. "I can put down two dishes of food and the guys will point with a paw toward the one they prefer."

The others laughed and the Colonel said, "Just imagine a Congress of Tigers that could actually make a decision."

"That could have a big impact on foreign policy too," the General chuckled. "Putin prefers leopards."

22

Quentin continued, "The guys are six out of six for picking high-protein sack food options. I went to the wholesale warehouse and got one of each item that looked promising. Can you believe they have Monkey Chow in a bag? Plus the Zoo aren't their only customers."

"I think my sister feeds that to my nephews," the General speculated. "Or at least she should. It's got to be cheaper and better for them than Fruit Loops and Lucky Charms."

"I was raised on puffed wheat that came from the Commissary in a bushel sack," the Colonel related. "We moved from base-to-base until I went off to the Academy. I never got within ten feet of a Fruity Pebble until I was twenty-two and was so conditioned by then that they smelled too gross to dare put in my mouth."

"It was pillow-sized shredded wheat for us, not the frosted minis," the General added. "My father ate his with a knife and fork, insisting his sons do the same. We didn't know you could attack them with a spoon until we were in high school, convinced this was an urban legend, less credible than Elvis taking a selfie with Sasquatch and Nessie in a phone booth."

* * *

So far the tigers mostly stayed at Booth's home, which was out on Long Island and somewhat rural. There was a large backyard with a high fence that had come with the house, as the previous owner had been somewhat of a celebrity and valued her privacy. When Booth was out of town on a worksite and his wife needed a break from two extra very furry kids to manage, Quentin would take Ravi and Tavi with him and stay at his folks place out on Staten Island. It too was rural enough to hide the guys.

Quentin continued his efforts with the sewer rats but with less urgency. He also focused on more quantitative details, as he had before with the single-cell organisms and water samples. These became tables and graphs with text in the growing Dissertation. The longer drives back-and-forth to Long Island consumed more of his day but did provide time with the radio, which inevitably lead to more yearning for Ann and the emotional rollercoaster. To distract himself from these sad musings, he would contrive situations in which the tigers might attract unwanted attention and how he might best diffuse each possible situation. For certainly, each passing day meant ultimately drawing closer to an unavoidable confrontation which would involve someone who might put down the big proverbial foot and stop the Project.

Quentin couldn't let that happen and so he must climb the next stair. That meant finding a suitable blind candidate who would work with Ravi and prove the idea of using the tigers for a guide and protector. The Colonel was exploring the possibility of using a disabled warrior who had lost vision but the Veterans' Administration was proving to be a convoluted snarl of conflicting objectives and dizzying rules. She had considered putting out the word and contacting one of these directly but the fussy Administrator of that Program at the VA absolutely forbid her to do this and threatened to blow the whole thing up if she did. If ever Quentin had considered the Military as a career, these experiences more than adequately proved his temperament was unsuitable.

Chapter 7. The Surprise

The morning after Quentin showed up with Ravi, Ann awoke with the alarm clock. As she reached over to silence it, her hand brushed across Ravi's large paw. He was poised, ready for her day to begin. He followed her to the bathroom and waited patiently for her to shower, always careful to position himself beside—not in—her path. She poured a bowl of cereal for herself before remarking, "I bet you'd like a little something too." She opened the cabinet and one of the new bags of food toppled out. "I may need to get you a bigger bowl." After figuring out how to unzip the bag and reaching for the scoop in the old bag, Ann filled the dog dish, wondering...

This stuff reminds me of hamburger helper... Probably costs a fortune... Good thing Quentin is bringing more. This is just so strange... It can't be a coincidence that some guy I haven't seen in years shows up with a replacement guide at the very moment I need one and none are available. Same old Quentin... shy... awkward... self-effacing... so apologetic. I wish he would share his feelings with me—about me. Am I just a friend? Is it more than that? If it is, why doesn't he say something. Can anyone possibly be that clueless?

Toby's harness wasn't nearly big enough to fit around Ravi's chest. "You are such a big boy," she said teasingly. "If anyone attacks me, you can just sit on them until they say, 'Uncle'." Ann got one of her belts out of the closet but even that wasn't big enough. Two belts buckled end-to-end did the trick.

They were out the door and onto the sidewalk, headed to the radio station where she worked as a DJ. Twenty-four hours before Ann had wondered when she would make it to the Station and who would have to take her there. Getting a cab or Uber twice a day would break the budget and feel helpless—something the feared more than a flock of purse-snatchers. If there was one thing that defined her life goal it was self-sufficiency everywhere and at all times. "The lack of physical sight will *not* stop me!" was her motto.

At that moment a woman shrieked, brakes screeched, and two men shouted what could only be a curse in some foreign language common to cabbies in New York City. As she neared the end of the block, there was more yelling, followed by what might have been someone trying to climb inside a mailbox through the letter flap—such are the images that flash through the mind of the blind. Further down the block approaching the crosswalk, Ann and her guide encountered more terrified screaming and tires screeching. This time there were two loud 'thumps', indicating a three-car collision. The wreck must have been near or in

25

the crosswalk, as Ravi led his charge across the street in a curved path, avoiding some unseen obstacle.

The chaos continued for five more blocks until they arrived at the bus stop. The front door opened and a woman screamed. The front door shut and the back door opened. Ann heard the woman exit at the rear and scurry off like a scared mouse. The back door closed and Ann called out, "Hey! I need on, please!" But the bus just roared off, leaving the two of them standing there at the curb.

Ann threw up her hand in exasperation and began the eighteen-block walk to the Station. Two blocks into the chaos she asked Ravi, "Have the aliens landed or has everyone gone nuts?" Ann was more annoyed than curious but Ravi seemed to take it all in stride—literally. Along the way they encountered what might have been a mute policeman who could only communicate with his whistle and was ordering the aliens to get back in their spaceship this very instant and leave this galaxy forever!

Eventually, the two arrived at the back door to the Station in the alley, as this was the shortest distance along the path from the Apartment. Ann opened the door with the swipe card and they climbed the stairs to the third floor, where her little office sat in a windowless corner of the building. All the other rooms on the hall were storage. The Studio was around the corner on the front side of the building, which had a minimal view of the Street so that the sighted staff could at least tell if it was pouring rain outside, though the weather report was contracted out and came from another facility. Ann wasn't scheduled to be on the air until noon, when they began taking calls and switched over to the afternoon programming. There were always two DJs and two technicians in the Studio 24/7.

Ann plopped into the chair, leaned back, and stroked Ravi. "Well, that was an adventure! I can't promise we'll have this much excitement every day. My life is usually pretty boring."

At that moment Tonya Franklin rounded the corner and gasped. Ann responded, "What?"

"Has it had breakfast?" Tonya pleaded.

"Yes, of course, he's on a special diet."

"I bet he is and I hope I'm not it."

"He's a real sweetheart."

"Are you sure it's not a sweet tooth?"

"He's a lot bigger than Toby."

"Girl, you have no idea what you have curled up at your feet, do you?"

"They told me it might be six months before I could get a replacement for Toby but out of the blue this blast from my past shows up with Ravi here."

"Blast from the past? Was it Christopher Robin, Winnie the Pooh, or Eeyore?"

"He's more like Eeyore—really shy and nerdy. What are you talking about?"

"That ain't no guide dog!"

"He's soft as a cat but, of course, cat's don't get this big."

"That kind do!"

"What kind?"

"Ravi is *Tigger*—literally, a tiger," Tonya explained.

"You can't be serious," Ann balked. "An actual tiger?" As she felt around the big cat's face and recalled the huge paws, the truth slowly sunk in. "I guess that explains all the screaming and why they wouldn't let us on the bus."

"I'm surprised they let you in the City."

"A policeman did whistle his head off, as we passed by."

"Let me get this straight," Tonya continued. "Some guy from your past shows up with a *tiger* to replace your guide *dog* and neglects to mention the difference?"

"He isn't the most expressive guy but he did insist that I would never be mugged again."

"I guess not! When word gets out, every mugger in town will be gone like the wind."

"He did mention that barking wouldn't be a problem," Ann added and began to laugh at the utter absurdity of the situation.

Tonya relaxed a bit, less fearful of becoming Ravi's breakfast. "You gotta wonder, where does a guy get a tiger that's leash-trained and doesn't eat everyone in sight?"

"Oh, Ravi's more than just leash-trained," Ann explained. "He can fetch things and obey all sorts of commands plus he led me around what must have been a three-car wreck that we caused."

"OK... Maybe the circus went out of business and Ravi got downsized."

"Perhaps... If he wasn't used to being in a cage, to just dump him at the zoo would be a real bummer."

"What's this guy's name?"

"Quentin," Ann replied. "I sat on him in high school."

"I think you told me that story," Tonya laughed.

"Yes, who could forget it? At the time I wondered if he liked me but he never said anything. The fact that he showed up at my apartment at just the right time with just what I needed is sort of creepy."

27

"He must have been stalking you all this time."

"He's not like any stalker I've ever heard of."

"I guess so... If he were going to do something creepy like in the movies, he would have done it already."

"He was almost crying several times while introducing Ravi, explaining his bags of special food that smell like hamburger helper—I guess we know why that is now—and reassuring me that everything would be OK. I think he does really like me and always has, just can't get up the courage to say it." Ann conceded.

"I think you're into something big here," Tonya agreed.

Chapter 8. The Collar

"You can't have a dangerous animal in the City!" the police officer screamed again, his pistol shaking.

"He's not dangerous," Ann pleaded. "He's a sweetheart. Pet him and shake his paw if you don't believe me."

"Drop the leash and step away!" the Animal Control officer demanded.

"You'll have to shoot me first," Ann said defiantly, dropping to the sidewalk and draping herself over the tiger.

"Fine!" the Animal Control officer roared. "I will tranquilize *both* of you."

A smartly-dressed woman who was standing on the sidewalk nearby watching this conflict unfold spoke with authority. "Gentlemen, I suggest you inspect the collar."

"Just stay out of this," the police officer snarled. "We can handle it."

"Clearly, you can't," she replied.

An old man with a Vietnam War Veteran's cap, who was edging closer by this point, peered over the girl and beast to get a closer look. "Jumping Jehoshaphat, will you look at that!" he exclaimed.

"What?" the Animal Control officer balked.

"Marine Corps," the old man explained.

Ann lifted Ravi's collar to clear it of fur and the police officer read aloud, while the Animal Control officer trembled.

Sgt. R. Tiger, USMC (703) 545-6700

"Will you call or shall I?" the woman insisted.

"I'll do it," the Animal Control officer reluctantly agreed.

"Hello, Pentagon, how may I direct your call?"

"Uhh... We have a tiger here with your phone number on his collar."

"That would be Sergeant Ravi Tiger?"

"I guess so..."

"And your reason for calling?"

"He's on the sidewalk here in New York."

"That's right. His current assignment is there."

"Assignment?"

"Yes, Sergeant Tiger is on active duty at this time."

"He can't be here in the City. He should be in a zoo."

29

"That's our decision, not yours."
"I'm fixin' to tranq him and take him to the Zoo."
"No you're not! You don't have jurisdiction."
"Let me talk to your boss. I'll just take this higher up."
"This goes all the way up. Stand down!"
"Like all the way to City Hall?"
"No, like all the way to the Whitehouse!"
click...

The Woman looked the Animal Control officer in the eyes and insisted, "Are we done here?"

"I can't just walk away and let a man-eater roam the streets," he protested, looking to the Cop for support, who shrugged and returned the gun to its holster, but kept his hand at the ready just in case.

"I think you most certainly can and will," the Woman asserted. "Clearly this particular one is not a *man*-eater, as you suggest."

"But what if it does eat someone?"

"Then the Marine Corps can handle it."

"Won't that be too late?"

"That's clearly not your concern."

"He's not going to eat anyone," Ann pleaded. "Unless they attack me. If they snatch my purse, he'll just take their arm off and keep it to chew on in the evenings when we're relaxing."

"This isn't a joking matter!" the Animal Control officer stammered.

"I'm sure that anyone stupid enough to attack me won't think Ravi is the slightest bit funny."

The Woman got in the back of a long black town car with darkly tinted windows. Two black SUVs—one ahead and one behind—sat poised at the curb. The three vehicles hastily pulled away in choreographed unison. The Animal Control and police officers both took note of this, thinking she was most certainly in charge of something big. Even the Mayor's entourage paled in comparison. The Vet let out a long, low whistle and said, "That one probably runs the FBI or the CIA or some other acronym we ain't supposed to know exists."

Ann stood and Ravi with her, straightened herself, grasped his harness, shouldered her bag, tapped the red-and-white stick, and sallied forth with an air of satisfaction. The two officers sulked away and the Vet watched them go.

Ann stopped at the Greek Café and picked up the dinner she had ordered earlier, then began the long walk home. As she encountered people and heard their gasps of fear, she called out reassuringly, "It's OK. He only eats purse-snatchers—otherwise very friendly. Feel free to pet him."

A few people did stop and one ventured to touch. From the voice, she guessed this was an older man with a noticeable Greek accent. "You know..." he began. "Alexander da Great had a pair uh these dat he got from India for being nicey-nicey and not burning the place down. Dey used to sleep with him too. Like for protection, you know. Of course, dey poisoned him anyway. Not the tigers, but da guy. Two big stone tigers are still around somewhere. This guy looks like he will keep you safe too, not like that girl who got smacked in the Subway last week."

"That was me," Ann said.

"Yikes! That ain't gunna happen again."

They continued on their separate ways and she pondered this new situation... Safety at last... Never again vulnerable... Quentin had said it with such certainty. No wonder... She hadn't realized the significance at the time but that's exactly what he meant and why. His bringing her this remarkable "solution" to her problems—not only a replacement guide but also a lethal protector—had been no coincidence. Indeed... this was no accident. Not that she thought Quentin capable of snatching her purse, pushing her down, and clubbing her dog just to create an excuse to gift her a tiger, but still... The close call, the near miss, the urgency opened a door and the super shy guy who wouldn't make a move before literally rushed through to rescue her.

Where he got the tiger was a different question but that he was there on the doorstep at the right moment was undeniable. That he was obviously nervous and reluctant, but pushed ahead anyway was clear. She momentarily thought back on the relationship that never was and briefly wondered if it might ever be, then quickly diverted her thoughts to where Quentin might have gotten Ravi. This was a much safer topic.

He was always into environmental things and saving the Planet. Maybe the idea hit him and he called up the Big Cats rescue place. "Hey, you guys got a spare kitty that could double as a guide dog for a blind girl up here in The City?" She imagined the conversation. The ones at the Zoo aren't trained in the complexities of maneuvering through obstacles, when to sit and where. They might have everything else under the Sun, but you can't just order a trained tiger from Amazon. No, that was all way too unlikely. It had to be a coincidence. He knew someone with a trained tiger looking for a job and blind girl in need of one. Just a coincidence. After all, someone does win the lottery. The winning number just might be Aunt Matilda's birthday and anniversary.

"'There is no such thing as coincidences,' is just something people say who have no imagination. Right?" She said aloud to Ravi, who gave a little shrug, which could be felt through the harness. Did he just respond to my question, she wondered. He was remarkably smart. She talked to Toby all the time but he never replied or gave an opinion of his own.

31

At that moment an old woman emitted a strange noise and stumbled off the sidewalk onto the street, kicking a can that made a noise giving Ann a direction. "Sorry. He's a good boy. Not to worry. He won't hurt you," she added as the woman scurried away.

Chapter 9. The Chat

"This is Ann at WNYG-FM, Totally Uplifting Radio with your favorite songs plus another reminder to Quentin that we *must* have a little chat and I promise not to bite."

That evening Ann sat on the couch running her toes through Ravi's fur listening to an audible book by her favorite author, J. B. Dudley, about a sweet innocent little waitress who was poisoning rude people as a service to the community. The Detective, who absolutely hated working murder cases but was on loan from Burglary because the Homicide guy was out with hemorrhoids, was devouring a plate of Chicken Fettuccini Alfredo and pouring forth his lament to none other than the culprit, whom he wouldn't suspect in a million years and who listened with sincere empathy.

"Did you save room for cheesecake tonight?" she asked.

"No," he sulked. "I've got to chase down some leads on these latest poisonings. It seems the only thing linking the victims is that nobody liked them. Everyone I have interviewed so far is glad they're dead and would like to thank whoever did it."

The door buzzer emitted its familiar sound and Ann rose to answer it. The door was open just a crack when Quentin burst forth with apologies. "I am so sorry... so very sorry... I just had to do something. I couldn't stand another moment thinking you were in danger. I wish it had been me in the Subway. I would give anything to have prevented that from happening. I knew Ravi would be the ultimate protector. I promise he won't eat you. He's super smart and if he got anything from my DNA it would be love for you." With this said, Quentin fairly collapsed sobbing.

Ann took his arm and helped him into the Apartment. "Sit on the couch and we can talk."

"Well, that answers one question," she thought to herself. "Love. At last he said it."

"Trust me," Quentin pleaded. "Ravi is super smart and not like any other... except his twin, Tavi. They were embryos together, which is how this whole thing started—The tiger thing, not the you-and-me thing... If that *is* a thing... Which I *hope* it is... But it's OK if you're not interested... I mean, of course, you can keep Ravi even if you toss me out... I won't hold it against you... I could *never* hold anything against you, of course... I mean figuratively, of course... The holding it against you thing—"

"Hush," she whispered, touching her finger to his lips. "It's OK. Just stop talking. Take some deep breaths and relax. Why don't you start at the beginning—How you came to have two smart tigers, not the beginning when I sat on you." This produced a little laughter and lightened the mood enough for Quentin to ease off the proverbial ledge.

"So... I went to Uni to study genetics but also wanting to do something about the environment. They're so picky and hyper-focused," Quentin began and Ann thought, "Look who's talking."

"Well... I went to a lecture and got hooked up with this guy, Dr. Booth, who is an adjunct professor and works on environmental clean-up projects for the Department of Defense. Wow! They've got some doozies to deal with. At least they have some people who are trying to save the Planet in all of it. He discovers this very rare chemical—from another mess—that can be used to cut-and-splice DNA. We both hope that it can eventually be used to repair the DNA in some endangered species. The cheetah and giant panda are two at risk, not for lack of habitat but for the accumulated genetic burden."

"This is the old Quentin I know," Ann thought. "Rambling on about technical stuff I can barely understand."

"We can't experiment on an endangered species. We must first prove and refine the technique before risking them. Things didn't go well for the rats. Let's not discuss the details," Quentin's voice quavered at this point, but he pressed on.

"Then this opportunity popped up: A pair of tiger embryos were going to be discarded because they might have thawed, split, and refrozen due to some problem with the cryofridge. The process of bringing them to life is so expensive that the Zoo wasn't willing to risk it, fearing there might be something serious wrong with them. The Professor and I were, of course, more than willing. He just squeezed it into his existing budget and so the DoD paid the bill. His golden retriever, Auro, gave birth to them and loved them like her own puppies."

"Then someone at the Pentagon found out we were genetically modifying tigers and they were paying for it. It supposedly stopped everything and almost caused a national emergency until this other person suggested we give one of them to Darcy, the President's daughter, as a guide, figuring she could talk them down off the ledge and get things back on track."

"I've heard about her," Ann interjected. "She really has a mind of her own—kind of like someone else I know. So that's the 'Darcy' you let slip before."

"Yes, and she is totally onboard with the plan. She loves Tavi and can hardly wait for the Secret Service to agree, however begrudgingly."

"How are Ravi and Tavi genetically-modified?" Ann questioned.

"I spliced in some of my own DNA," Quentin reluctantly admitted. "I didn't want to risk any other animals. It just seemed like the logical thing to do."

"Well," Ann chuckled. "I think it worked because he exhibits some of your behavior, is very smart, and I suspect is also particularly fond of me."

Quentin squirmed... and Ann considered... Should they have the DTR talk or not? Was this too soon? After several moments of silence, she decided to put that bigger 'chat' off to a later date. Date... was this a date? Change the subject... before he runs screaming into the darkness.

"Let's talk about school," Ann began. "Uni was too expensive so I went to Galverton and got an associates degree in communication. I had a head start on that one. Then I got a certificate in radio broadcasting. I have listened to WNYG for years. They interviewed me after the first mugging. I really hit it off with the Reporter and she got me an interview with the Station Manager. Three weeks later I was on the air talking about the latest songs, a little news, a few world events, and living the dream. I can almost afford this apartment if I don't eat anything."

"I'll supply Ravi's food," Quentin injected nervously. "You won't have to pay for that—or anything else, like vet bills. We—I mean *he*—won't be a burden. I promise. Cross my heart and hope I die."

"I'm just kidding," Ann said soothingly. "My parents help out and I may get a raise in a year or two. It's just living in the City that's so crazy expensive. I don't qualify for subsidized housing or any kind of financial assistance. I'm not sure I'd take it, even if I did qualify. I want to do this thing on my own."

Ann could almost feel Quentin cringe and imagined him now in the fetal position so that she added. "I'm not saying that I want to always be alone, of course. Just that I relish the feeling of accomplishment—especially achieving things that many of the blind never do."

After a somewhat uncomfortable pause Ann prodded, "Now you tell me a story... about your school experience."

"I got right in to Uni. I never applied anywhere else. I never thought to. When I got there, so many other students went on-and-on about all the schools they applied to and how long it took to hear back and how they had to match the school with the scholarship and all the hassle. After twenty-two courses, I got a bachelor's in genetics. I had already been working in the Laboratory and talking with the professors so staying on seemed like the thing to do. I filled out some forms and sooner than I expected, I got a master's."

"Long about this time I ran into Booth at the lecture. We really hit it off. He got me signed up for a doctorate and stepped in to be my advisor and square it all up with the rest of the faculty. We had this project and the DoD was paying for it. When the embryos became available, it was like a dream come true. I've been so focused on Ravi and you that I haven't made any progress on my

35

dissertation but I'll get back to it eventually. We can cut-and-splice DNA but haven't yet figured out how to select which specific part to choose. Booth thinks the splicer, cyclodeclamide, is implicitly making the choice based on maximal affinity. In order to direct the choice, we must come up with another chemical—who knows what of the billion possibilities—to control the selection."

Ann was struggling a bit to keep up by this point, as Quentin continued unabated. "Booth has found this other rare chemical, bromo-tri-fluoro-benzene, at a new dump site that he thinks will be a game-changer. It's pretty nasty, but is in very small quantities and fairly easy to clean up. It doesn't cause defects but clings only to certain parts in the cell nucleus, which is promising."

"Dump site?" Ann inquired.

"I don't ask and he doesn't say, but apparently there are leaks and spills everywhere, especially at some military bases. They are scrambling to get them all cleaned up. Some are a bigger challenge than others. I get the impression that we've caught some other countries developing chemical and biological warfare agents and shut down their operations, probably brought samples back for analysis—that sort of thing. It's all rather hush-hush. I've met several of the people working on the projects and they all seem very dedicated to doing it right. Please don't mention it to anyone, especially on the air."

"I won't breathe a word," Ann promised. "It's good to know that people care about these things. I can see how the Press would just complicate an already difficult situation."

"Well, that went well," Ann thought after Quentin left. "I think we've got something special that just might grow into a relationship."

36

Chapter 10. The Bus

Not only did the bus driver stop and open the door for them, but shouts of welcome burst forth to greet them. It seems that after the television story about their encounter with Animal Control, which showed Ann draping herself over Ravi, to shield him from the tranquilizer darts aired, the driver's two grandsons couldn't wait to hug the tiger. The woman and the tiger climbed aboard to receive a hero's welcome. Ravi savored every moment. Clearly, some of the passengers hadn't seen the news or heard the story, but were soon convinced they were in no danger.

The boys wanted to take Ravi to show-and-tell at school and made a very convincing case for it. Ann did not make any promises but did think it would be a fun adventure and might lead to some conversations about challenges facing the blind and also safety in the City, especially on the Subway. Several passengers did comment that any purse-snatcher would indeed be a fool to mess with her now. One young woman said that she'd been accosted twice—not for her purse—and said, "If he has a brother, I'll feed him filet mignon seven days a week."

"The guy who had Ravi did say something about a twin but that he was already promised to someone named Darcy," Ann explained. "If I can ever get a hold of him, I'll ask. Who knows... maybe someone is raising them just for this job." Best to not share too many details...

The rest of the bus ride went well and Ann was relieved to have a shorter walk than on the previous several days. Ravi boarded and exited the bus like he did this all the time. Strange... Was there a guide school out there training tigers? Were all tigers this friendly with people or was it just domesticated ones? In order to domesticate a tiger do you start with kittens? Are tiger babies called kittens? Cubs just doesn't sound right. Cubs is OK for lions and bears but not tigers.

* * *

Later that evening on the sidewalk two blocks from the Station, they encountered the old Vet, who saluted and asked, "How is the Sergeant today?"

"He's very pleased with himself," Ann replied. "We got quite a reception on the bus. I think he's become a celebrity and it suits him quite well indeed."

"He seems to carry the responsibility well," the Vet observed. "Like he's been at this job for a while and not straight out of Boot Camp. How long have you had him?"

"Just three days," Ann explained. "He came fully trained. I don't know any of the details. The guy who provided him and I go back a way but he's not the talkative type and—get this—he forgot to mention that Ravi wasn't a dog. I didn't find out until I got to work."

"That's kinda hard to miss. Is he blind too?"

"No, but he is really shy."

"That's beyond shy. He's not like from another planet, I hope. I got some guys in the *know* who insist they've been here a long time—not just Roswell in '47. Like they were here building the Pyramids. They've got access to some mighty secret stuff. I could tell ya, but then I'd have to kill ya, sorta stuff."

"I think I heard that somewhere too, but..."

"You know Billy Gates is one of them, right?"

"I didn't know that."

"That's where the computer came from. He had one of them chips in his pacifier when they crashed," the Vet relayed, showing no signs of reaching a conclusion.

"That's all very interesting," Ann apologized. "I've got to catch my bus." Ravi sensed her desire to disengage from this dizzying conversation and so they fairly trotted down the block and away from alien territory.

* * *

The evening bus driver was up to speed on the news and let them aboard but was not talkative and didn't bring any grandchildren to greet Ravi. There were usually only a few on this bus at this time. Only one passenger gasped. Ann imagined the others not looking up from their papers or staring straight ahead in the usual New York City mass transit trance of disconnection.

Before long they arrived at the Apartment. Ann poured a bowl of food for Ravi, again noting the "aroma" of hamburger helper, which produced a chuckle this time. She then warmed a dish of leftover pork lo mein for herself. She sat down to eat and told Alexa to resume the audio book where they had left off the night before.

The sweet little Waitress was serving a family of five. The Mom looked harried and disheveled. The little Boy looked down at the table and pouted. The Baby sat in the booster seat, smearing food everywhere. The little Girl wouldn't make eye contact and had bruises on her face and arm. The Dad looked half-plastered and like he just got off from digging ditches.

The Waitress asked if there was anything else they might like, desert perhaps. "A shot of vodka would be nice," the Dad snapped.

The Mom started to say, "Please don't..." The Dad raised his hand to strike her but the Waitress interrupted, "Sorry, we only have beer."

38

With caustic reluctance, the Dad said, "I guess that'll have to do."

The Waitress scurried off to the kitchen to get the beer. After making certain that no one was watching, she withdrew the little vial from her pocket and tapped five drops into the glass. She then placed it down before the Dad and softly said to the Mom, "Trust me. Things will be better very soon."

The grumpy old Detective was just two tables away and never suspected a thing, but there would be another dead body before the night was over. The Waitress placed a slice of raspberry cheesecake before the Detective and said soothingly, "You look exhausted. Eat this. It will make you feel better."

* * *

The next morning the bus driver extended the condolences of his grandsons that they couldn't skip school again but sent pictures they had drawn of Ravi, Ann, and themselves—one on a bus and another beside a tree. He reiterated their invitation to visit school but did say they hadn't asked the Teacher if this would be OK.

When they were rolling, a guy seated across and slightly toward the rear said, "Nice tiger. What does he eat? Like fried chicken by the bucket? Wait... Don't tell me... Frosted Flakes?"

"Not that I know of," Ann laughed. "That's his cousin Tony."

"Ha! Good one."

A gal slightly toward the front said, "I got an Ex I'd like him to eat. You don't do chomp out orders, do you?"

"That would like totally be a big business," the guy guffawed.

"I guess you're the one we saw on the news that got mugged and upgraded to a tiger," the gal suggested.

"Yes, that's me. He's quite an upgrade: scary and smart too."

"Ain't nobody going to touch you now!" the guy exclaimed. "Else they be catnip or Frosted Flakes."

The three were laughing and Ravi was enjoying the banter when someone emitted a little 'harrumph' from directly across the aisle, which silenced them. After a brief pause, a scratchy old woman's voice said, "It's just not safe having a wild animal on the loose, prowling around the streets at night looking for someone to eat. It's bad enough, what with all the gypsies, tramps, and thieves we have now, to add a vicious beast."

"He's not vicious or a beast and he stays with me all the time," Ann said reassuringly.

"He might eat the thieves," the guy supposed. "Hopefully not the tramps and gypsies, of course."

39

"Still, it's just not safe!" the old crone insisted.

"He looks safe to me," the gal added.

Much to Ann's relief, the bus stopped and they got off.

Chapter 11. The Ninja

Darcy strategically placed the three trackers she had removed—two from her sneakers and one from the dog's collar—on the dresser and bedside table, grasped Scooby's harness, and slipped down the hall to the back stair at the Whitehouse. She carefully opened the special window with the defective sensor, slipped out, and closed it softly. She crept along the back side of the building before darting across the lawn so as to not attract attention to her escape route. The night was dark in a new moon, not that this mattered to a blind girl or her dog. When they were five hundred yards away she began to breathe more easily.

"Ninja is on the move," the radio crackled. "Repeat. Ninja is on the move!"

"That's a negative. GPS has her upstairs asleep."

"Check again, guys! She's given you the slip."

Secret Service Agents Marks, Milton, and Mearns or 3M as they were known, sat in the kitchen sipping coffee and watching the Bills vs. Chiefs game from earlier in the day. It was two in the morning and all was quiet in the Whitehouse—or so they thought, but they were wrong. Their "charge" had just done a runner and snuck out on them again—the third time this month. When not watching sports, they would speculate what each of them had done wrong or who they had offended so as to be assigned to the night shift watching the "kid". This particular kid-watching Team—whether day or night, weekday, weekend, or holiday—could be distinguished from the rest of Secret Service—who always wore nicely polished leather shoes—by their sneakers. The necessity for this wardrobe exception was clear as the moment at hand, for the three jumped up from the table and dashed off in different directions, as previously discussed in preparation for this inevitable development.

Twenty-two minutes and thirty-five seconds later Milton stopped running, bent over, grasped his knees, and took deep breaths—after checking his watch, of course. When he had recovered enough to speak, he grasped the radio. "Got her at the far end of the Pool. Head over to the Mall. No rush."

Agent Milton strode up to the dog and girl, who was dangling her feet over the edge. He was still breathing somewhat heavily, as he spoke. "How's the water this evening?"

"It's a little too chilly for a swim," she replied.

"Good, I didn't bring my swimsuit."

"You're going to get us fired," he chided. "We have families to feed and rent to pay."

41

"You don't have to report it," she suggested.

"I'm not sure which would get us in more trouble—that you slipped past us or that we didn't report it."

"Scooby, what do you think we should do about this?"

"Woof!"

"Of course he's going to agree with you," Milton added.

"I just feel like a bird in a cage," Darcy explained. "I can't stand being cooped up. I want to be free."

"Yeah, I get that," Milton agreed. He sat and they waited for Marks and Mearns to arrive.

* * *

As Darcy sat on the edge of the pool she pondered life. Scooby was still panting from their walk, which was just over a mile. He was getting old and his joints hurt. His hearing was going too. He would soon retire. The Group assured her that he would go to a good home where he could rest and be appreciated. She would get a new guide: Tavi the Tiger. That was exciting but also sad. Life rolls on whether you want it to or not. You gotta go with the flow or drown.

There were few sounds on the Mall this night in addition to a little road noise in the distance. It was much more chaotic during the daylight hours. She liked this place, though their home in Vermont was so much better than Washington. Her father was nearing the end of a second term and so they would soon be leaving the 'fussel and bussel' as she called it, behind. She rarely made a public appearance since arriving in DC. It was just so upsetting and useless. No one ever seemed to do anything remotely like *progress* in this place. According to Mom, Dad aged a decade for each year in this job she had pleaded with him to refuse, but the Party *needed* him, and so he stepped up to the proverbial plate, as he always did.

Once again Darcy considered the various senses. Most people thought the loss of sight was the worst, but she put it second or third. Arranging sound, smell, and touch in priority was a challenge. She thought of those who could never again smell a roast or casserole or cake fresh out of the oven after having COVID. How sad... To never feel anything again would be horrible. She stroked Scooby and thought of children in Africa with leprosy. To never hear a bird sing would be the worst. She was thankful for her ears, nose, and fingers that worked. Being blind wasn't all that bad.

* * *

Agent Milton sat on a nearby bench, rather than dangling his feet in the water. He too pondered life. He had always dreamed of being an FBI agent but that never seemed to be an option. He made all the right moves, as recommended, got the right training and filled out the right forms but it just didn't happen. "Can someone *please* explain why?" He had asked more times

42

than he cared to remember. The nearest thing to an answer he had ever gotten was, "You don't check enough boxes." To which he protested, "What exactly does that mean?"

He eventually got onboard with the Secret Service, which was not nearly as exciting as it sounds. After whining about yet another seemingly useless assignment, another agent had said, "At least you aren't assigned to watch the very ancient former President Jimmy Carter sleep in his wheelchair and dribble food down his shirt. I got that one for eighteen months and was ready to jump off the nearest bridge. Trust me, it could be a lot worse."

Yet another agent said she had been on Air Force One three times and didn't get so much as a peanut-free-cracker. "The Press sit in the front with the 'important' people while we're packed in the tail with the baggage. I had to sit on the floor for fifteen hours squashed between two food carts that smelled like the market in Hunan where they sell sautéed scorpions and dead bats. It was about the time COVID arrived and may be how it got here."

* * *

Eventually, Marks and Mearns arrived and the four walked slowly back to the Whitehouse, talking as they went. This had become routine with Darcy sneaking out at least one night each week. There was no real harm in it and this was better than standing in the background scanning a crowd for possible shooters or rotten tomato tossers while the Big Cheese delivered some boring speech about the urgency of colonizing Mars, cooling the Earth to combat Global Warming, bringing jobs back to America while limiting robots on the assembly line, and promising that Social Security and Medicare would be there forever and always.

"The expression, 'difference between night and day,' sure applies to this place," Marks remarked. "Chaos and noise by day with relative quiet and calm by night."

"Oh, I'm sure that up around K-Street there are plenty of drunks staggering out of the pubs weeping over the ball game or singing the victory song," Mearns added.

"I'm pretty sure my little brother is there now, collecting bets and making toasts," Milton sighed. "Life is one big party for him and always has been. I never have understood how it is that he checks all the boxes and I never do. First year working for a pharmaceutical company and he makes Salesman of the Year. Before you know it, he's Lobbyist of the Year, if there is such a thing."

"Growing up is tough," Darcy interjected. "I really appreciate everything you guys do. I hope you know that."

Mearns said, "We fuss all the time but we really love this job and we'd much rather hang out with you than deal with some of the other stuff around here."

43

"Your folks are OK," Marks quickly added. "It's not them that's the problem. "

"It's the bureaucracy," Milton added.

"Don't I know it," Darcy concluded.

Chapter 12. The Date

"So where are we going?" Ann inquired, as Quentin started the engine.

"7-7-6 which, according to my Grandmother, has the best Italian food this side of the Atlantic," he explained. "They don't waste time coming up with a catchy name or putting up a sign. They also don't waste time or money on menus. You're supposed to know what you can order in a *real* Italian restaurant."

"If I order the wrong thing will they kick me out?"

"Probably."

"What if I mispronounce Pomodoro or Melanzane or Pannacotta?"

"I think you'll do just fine. If there's any doubt, Ravi will protect you."

"Should I order Beef Tagliata for Ravi?"

"He loves it! I got it for him last time we were here."

"That's a relief," Ann sighed. "I was worried he would scare off all their customers."

"Oh, he and Tavi have been regulars there for months," Quentin explained.

"I still can't believe you've been able to keep one tiger a secret, let alone two. I presume you all don't romp through Central Park."

"Oh, no, we—Booth and I—have mostly kept them away from the Inner City, out on Long Island, where it's more rural. People are shocked but after the boys sit and offer to shake a paw, most warm up to the idea."

"So tell me more about this DNA thing."

"Ultimately, we want to be able to target the cut-and-splice process. We can sort of do that now but not with any particular end in mind, like fixing damaged DNA, which is often the problem with endangered species. If it were as simple as hatching out a batch in the lab and releasing them into the wild, they wouldn't be endangered. There are other species that reproduce so fast they will take over a habitat and push all the others out."

"You said that you spliced some of *your* DNA into Ravi," Ann prodded. "Does he have your eyes or smile perhaps?"

"No, not really," Quentin replied. "But he is quite smart is very interested in our conversation right now."

Ravi was indeed practically sitting on the console between the two front seats, turning his head back-and-forth as the two talked.

"So he has your brain but without all the *shy*," Ann laughed. "Nicely spliced!"

This comment about being *shy* made Quentin a little nervous but this was brief, as they had reached the Restaurant."

Ann got out and Ravi push into the front and out the door after her, anxious to get at the Beef Tagliata, no doubt.

* * *

They were welcomed by the Hostess and seated. Ann asked for a small glass of the house white wine but Quentin and Ravi opted for water. Orders were placed and several patrons came by to rub the tiger and say, 'hi'. This was followed by a little silence, which Ann eventually broke. "So... you obviously have kept up with me, where I work, and my apartment. Just admit it and we can move on to the next step."

Ann could almost feel Quentin trembling across the table. "It's OK. We don't need to have the DTR conversation tonight. It's always best to be honest. Just take your time. There's no pressure and I will support you regardless."

After a little more silence, Quentin finally mumbled, "Ever since the moment you *sat* on me... well, maybe a few moments *after* that, when I realized you were *blind* and it was an accident. It's OK that you're blind. I didn't mean it like that and it's OK that you *sat* on me. It's OK if you sit on me again. I mean, if it happens and I do something stupid and you *fling* yourself at me. Uhh... I don't mean it in that way. Not the flinging part, just the sitting part... it will be OK. Feel free to sit on me any time—any time at all. Sit as long as you like. Or stand... either way, it's OK with me."

"It's OK," Ann interrupted. "I won't sit on you at least until we finish dinner, of course. I might let you kiss me on the cheek later but no sitting on our first date."

"Really?!" Quentin gasped. "That would be so amazing! I mean... I'm OK with that, if you are, of course. It would be OK. Sure. No problem."

Well... That answers Question Number One: He's always had a crush on me. He didn't exactly come out and say it, but there's no doubt about it. He's been waiting all this time for an excuse to step back into my life. Question Number Two also answered. Having a spare tiger ready to drop off on my doorstep was just a coincidence and not an orchestrated conspiracy to free animals from the Zoo.

The food came and it was delicious. "Grandma was right. This is the best Italian food this side of the Ocean." Quentin and Ravi chomped and slurped and enjoyed their meals. Quentin relaxed enough during the meal that Ann could sense it.

46

They returned to the car. No furtive kiss on the cheek yet. Ann was determined they would not ride home in silence. It might take a while, but she would pry Quentin out of his shell eventually. "Tell me more about your research."

Hopefully, this will get him talking.

"So it all started with these single-celled organisms. That's where Booth got the idea from. We did enough with them to lay the groundwork. Then I moved up to some insects, which are more hassle than I had imagined. I switched to worms, which refuse to reproduce on demand. Working with them would take forever to get anywhere. That basically leaves rodents, which are happy to breed much more often. I guess that's where the jokes about rats and rabbits come from."

He was talking and relaxing. The plan was working.

"I got some rats—mice, really—from a pet store and tried a few things but didn't get anywhere. They're too fragile. I think it's because they've been so inbred for pet stores that they're too far removed genetically from the more robust original state in the wild. That's when we got Booth's brother-in-law, Chuck, to capture real sewer rats. I went with him twice—to the sewers—for real! He knows a guy who works for the City and told us the best place to look. If you can believe it, just a quarter mile into the darkness—from Penn Station no less—is like Rat Heaven. It's literally crawling with them, like some apocalyptic movie. I expected to see Will Smith and the Zombies."

"I finally started having some success with the rats—which, by the way, are way friendlier than mice, in spite of how they are portrayed in the movies. This one batch I call Gen-CP are total couch potatoes. All they do is eat and sleep but they can smell a food truck in Queens. Maybe that gene came from my Grandmother of Italian restaurant fame."

"She can call them," Ann chimed in. "I can attest to that."

"The next batch I call Gen-TD for Table Dancer. Just switch on the music and they begin dancing. It's totally weird. They don't just run on the exercise wheel, they run around with each other like they're in a dance competition. That gene might come from my other Grandmother, who rumor has it, got drunk once and danced on a table when the World's Fair was here."

"Gen-TW for Twilight or the 'vampires' was a flop—not like the couch potatoes, just for lack of any useful progress. They sleep all day and stay up all night, regardless of the lights in the Lab. It's like they know when the Sun comes up and when it goes down and there's no fooling them. Chuck thinks some of the rats in the sewer do the same thing, so it's like a null result. The other ones from the sewer who are now in the Lab don't work this way, but these do."

"The last batch is Gen-TV, because they love watching television—except, get this, Wheel of Fortune. They absolutely refuse to watch it. They go nuts for America's Got Talent and Family Feud. They are huge fans of Steve Harvey. Turn on Wheel of Fortune and they head for the exercise wheel in disgust."

At last, they arrived at the Apartment. Ann opened the door, turned and faced the street. Ravi sat and the two waited. Nearly a minute passed before Quentin brushed his lips against her cheek, which barely qualified as a 'kiss' but was a start...

Chapter 13. The Swap

After three months with Ann, Ravi had more than adequately proven himself to Darcy and 3M, if not the rest of the Secret Service. It was time for the *Swap*. Scooby was getting stiffer and in more pain by the day. His retirement home was ready and so was Darcy. It would be sad to say goodbye to Scooby, but it was best for him. The day of the swap was all set and the Staff had been warned.

When the Day arrived, there were two big events going on at the Whitehouse. One event was with the Tea Party, which didn't turn out as planned. It seemed there was a miscommunication somewhere and, instead of preparing for a political discussion thing, it was somehow mistaken for a party in which tea and scones would be served, hosted by the First Lady. Needless to say, the Tea Party were more than disappointed, but that would soon get worse.

The other event was a meeting of labor union heads. This was also a huge mess due to another miscommunication. It seems that the manufacturing unions wanted to squeeze out imports and the dock worker unions wanted to boost imports. These two groups should never be in the same room at the same time, but they were. No lunch had been prepared, but the President was soon on the menu. The arguing quickly shifted to fried or barbeque?

When Quentin, Professor Booth, Ann, Ravi, and Tavi arrived to see Darcy, the President and First Lady slipped out of their respective messes and off to the safety of a corridor the other guests could never enter. They had a delightful greet-and-chat, which lasted almost two hours. By this time the unions and Tea Party had thrown up their hands and left—a success on several fronts.

Somehow word of the "swap" had gotten out and several animal rights groups had taken offense, some to having a wild animal in captivity and others to genetic meddling. These formed a line along the periphery of the Whitehouse beside the concrete barriers and had brought an assortment of signs. Quentin, Booth, Ann, the President, and the First Lady were all in some various state of alarm, but Darcy was not. She grasped Tavi's harness and went out to meet the protesters.

"Line up... no pushing or shoving... everyone gets a turn," Darcy announced. "Shake a paw. Get a big hug and make Tavi feel like the hero that he is." In minutes the protesters couldn't remember what they had come for—except the shake and hug, of course.

It didn't take long for most of the Whitehouse staff to welcome Tavi, though some insisted he was inappropriate and dangerous. Jokes about missing staff fluttered about. "Are you sure Mitch is sick and the tiger didn't eat him for lunch?" He soon became Rikki Tikki Tavi, the giant mongoose and protector against all serpents—large and small. Several ambassadors, two especially rude ones in particular, became meal suggestions. "Rikki Tikki could take care of Ms. Snooty-Pants and Mr. Big Britches."

Life settled into a new sort of normal for Darcy and Ann. Darcy was invited to speak to several groups, where she became the de facto spokesperson for the cause of genetic repair. "Instead of sitting around twiddling our thumbs, let's face these challenges head on with focused intent." To one group, who was particularly concerned with trash in the seas, she proposed a new approach, "Put a serial number on some of the plastic bottles. It' doesn't have to be all of them. Track where they go. When they show up in the environment, wash up on the beach, whatever, find out who purchased them. Then investigate how they came to be in the environment. Did someone dump the stuff? Did some cruise ship push them off the back deck? Did some slob leave them at the beach? Find a few, make an example, and others will take note. Do something positive. Don't just pout and fuss!"

After the talk, one young woman came up to further discuss the plan. "Here's the deal," she began. "We've already tried that. My Dad has a cousin who works for Glacier's Gift. They sell bottled water that's supposed to come from a ten-thousand-year-old glacier but actually comes through the Cleveland municipal water supply—the same stuff that runs out of the hose or fire hydrant. At least they filter it three times. It's clean enough, but nothing special. Anyway, they don't want to cooperate because their customers might pitch a fit and switch over to another supplier."

"Well then, we need to get sneaky," Darcy chuckled.

"I like this idea," the young woman perked up.

"We need to get someone on the inside who will put a dot on a bottle here and there, different colors, taking note of which truck they're loaded on. Anyone who works at a plant or distribution site could do it. It would take patience but we could narrow it down one step at a time. Eventually, there will be enough information to identify a trail. Presumably, it's only a few big pigs and not a whole lot of little ones. If it isn't the big guys, there's no way to apply sufficient pressure to stop it."

This very much pleased the young woman, who began plotting a new more sneaky effort to clean up this mess. "When we find the pigs, if they refuse to stop, we can just feed them to Tavi or at least suggest that they would make a delicious meal for him."

50

* * *

Tavi had a nose for trouble—in the good sense. He would sense something and then lead Darcy off to investigate. Twice in the same week he led her to someone who was weeping. The first was a woman secretary, who had just broken up after a long and stormy relationship. The second was a security guard whose daughter was dying of leukemia. "I should have gotten a degree in counseling," Darcy thought to herself. "Maybe I can take a course or two online. There is clearly a need for that expertise around here."

This got her to thinking... All the fuss and bother in this place is so *impersonal*. Tax-and-spend, push-and-shove, trade-and-borrow, import-and-export, here a bomb, there a bomb, people always talking about this-or-that but rarely about he or she—the children, the families, the moms, the dads, the people. She mentioned this at dinner and her folks agreed. "What shall we do?" they asked. "Let's be more intentional," Darcy suggested. "Let's start right now."

"How shall we do that?" Dad asked.

"Let's try to ask at least one person each day how they're doing personally," Mom proposed.

"We know Tavi can do that," Darcy added and they all agreed.

The next morning during the weekly meeting in the Oval office, the President noticed that the Surgeon General, Dr. Preston seemed distracted. After the meeting was adjourned, he called him aside and asked if everything was OK. The doctor hesitated before sharing, "I just got back from Walter Reed Medical Center. It seems like every time I get an update there is some new strange symptom presenting itself in our troops after foreign deployment. These show up months or years after returning. They're mostly neurological, though there is one batch that appears as a rash. We're scrambling to deal with these on top of all the emotional trauma. The staff is overwhelmed. I think we need a new approach to this."

"Do you have any ideas?" the President asked.

"As a matter of fact, I do," the SG replied. "My son is into computers and not likely to follow in my footsteps. He's all over this AI stuff and talks about it continuously. He can't understand why AI hasn't been applied to sift through all the information gathered during COVID to see what might be learned."

"That sounds reasonable," the President agreed. "We've discussed that before but all the different players plus HIPAA always squash every idea."

"If we stay within the VA and only consider our people," the SG explained. "We might be able to pull it off and learn something that will make a real difference."

"I like it! Put together a plan and bring it up when it's ready."

51

* * *

That night Darcy came into the kitchen where the three agents were sipping coffee and sampling the leftovers from the party on the lawn earlier that day, which did not include tea, and announced, "I can't sleep so I'm sneaking out to the Mall. Anyone up for a stroll?" They were and it was a pleasant evening. When they were outside Darcy said, "OK... We must each share something personal. This is unofficially self-care week. You have Tavi to thank for this. I'll start... Since I can't see the expression on people's faces, I often don't pick up the signal when those around me are upset. Tavi seems very attune to these things and is finding ways to let me in on what's happening. That's really exciting for me. Now someone else share a bit."

Agent Mearns began, "My kids are both in middle school and are so upset about these school shootings. They say the other kids are too and that some are so distracted they can't focus on school. I couldn't help thinking that if one security officer in each school had a trained tiger to patrol the halls, there would be a lot fewer shootings."

Chapter 14. The Subway

That morning Ann was due to speak at a school near the northern-most stop on the Subway. She had made this trip several times before, but with Toby. This would be her first ride on the Subway with Ravi and she was a little apprehensive. The turnstiles, waiting beside the track, boarding, finding a seat or handle to grasp, then the rocking and clacking, would it be upsetting? She wasn't sure and had never thought to ask Quentin if Ravi had ever been on the subway before.

Except for the usual occasional gasp and cry from a passer-by, it was surprisingly routine. It seems Quentin did think of most everything. Not surprising for someone with OCD. As the door closed and the train accelerated, she could hear passengers moving away. Then the voice of a little boy said, "I want to pet the big kitty."

"It's a tiger," a woman's voice corrected. "I'm not sure it wants to be petted."

Ann said, "Oh, he loves to be petted and hugged."

She could hear the two moving closer and felt Ravi move, as the little boy got acquainted. "His name is Ravi."

"You are a very big kitty," the little boy proclaimed.

As the train rumbled along, Ann could hear more rustling of passengers. Soon they were conversing. "I wish I had a tiger. I'd feel a lot safer."

"Tigger was always my favorite character," another voice said.

Another voice broke into rhyme...

The Wonderful thing about Tiggers;
Is Tiggers are wonderful things.
Tops are made out of rubber;
Their bottoms are made out of springs.
Their bouncey, trouncey, ouncey, pouncey
fun, fun, fun, fun, fun.
But the most wonderful thing about Tiggers;
Is I'm the only one.

This very much delighted the little boy and so the conversation swirled round-and-round, as some exited and more boarded. As they reached the last stop and the northern end of the Line, it was just the two of them. Ann spoke, listened, and answered questions about being blind and also about working in the radio broadcasting business. The ride back to the City Center was equally entertaining and they arrived in time for the first break of the afternoon show.

* * *

Two hours in, the Station got a call from a Desk Sergeant at the NYPD asking to speak to the Tiger Girl. "Hello, this is Ann and you're on the air!"

"We here at the Twelfth Precinct would like to thank you for riding the Subway this morning," the voice said.

"Why is that?"

"Three guys just turned themselves in," the Sergeant chuckled. "They're confessing to all sorts of crimes and—get this—begging we send them to Rykers Island and put them behind bars. One of them keeps asking, 'You're sure tigers can't swim, right? Please tell me they can't swim!'"

"I talked to several people on the Subway this morning," Ann explained, "but nobody like that."

"One of the guys swears the tiger recognized him and licked his chops like it was suppertime."

"We're glad to be of service," Ann replied.

"You sure made our day," the Sergeant said and ended the call.

Five minutes later another call came in... "The guys at the Fifth Precinct would really appreciate it if you could just take a little stroll through a row of warehouses here. We've got a real problem with drug deals going down. By the time our guys in blue show up, it's deserted but we know they are there somewhere."

Before this call ended another came in, this one a woman with panic in her voice. "My son has been missing for almost two days and the Police say they can't do anything until a case is opened and paperwork filed and a team assigned and whatever... If I bring you some of his clothes, could you *please* search? He was last seen at school but he never got on the bus and his best friend was sick that day and I don't know where else to start..."

The switchboard lit up and continued that way for the rest of the afternoon. Ann apologized on the air for not being able to ferret out criminals or effect search-and-rescue or lost-and-found. She felt sorry for these people and that helping them was beyond her means but it did bring awareness to larger problems in life and that perhaps some innovative solutions might be forthcoming. She thought again of the unusual circumstances Quentin had described for obtaining the tiger embryos. That was not likely to be repeated but, perhaps more importantly, could the same genetic modification be achieved or was it just luck? As far as she knew, the idea had not been tested. Even with more tiger embryos, could two more such remarkable animals be created? Were Ravi and Tavi the only two that would ever be? Quentin wasn't clear on this and, as it turned out, that's because he had no idea.

54

Ann wasn't the only one in the Subway that week. Quentin and Chuck were on the hunt for the biggest legend of them all: alligators. Ever since he was a child, Chuck dreamed of catching a gator in the sewer. The only confirmed case was an 8-foot alligator found in an East Harlem sewer on February 9, 1935. Since then the legend has lived on in the steamy mist of young boy's dreams. Chuck was determined and Quentin was... well... roped in, if we're being honest. Quentin was positive they would find no gators but was willing to raise another generation of rats, which they no doubt would find.

Five hours into the hunt Quentin was exhausted. Chuck practically jumped out of his boots when he caught sight of a tail that just might be a baby alligator on the other end. The two crept forward and eventually came to an enclosure that housed several electrical panels. There huddled atop a little pile of rubbish were two tiny gators plus a half-dozen babies. Quentin gasped and Chuck adjusted the light to get a better look.

These looked like tiny gators until the two men inched closer, when the adults arched their backs, raising some sort of fins. Oh... not gators after all... just some sort of lizard, probably Iguanas. Surprisingly, they did not all flee into the darkness but welcomed the human attention.

Chuck stooped and said, "I bet you guys are starving."

Even more astonishing, the Iguanas let Quentin and Chuck pick them up and rock the babies.

"They're clearly accustomed to people. Probably got dumped and left to starve. Let's take them home, give them some food, and a nice bed," Chuck suggested.

"I'm game if you are," Quentin added. "They're not alligators but they're another species to experiment with. Maybe we'll learn something."

Chuck's wife, Stephanie, soon found homes for the babies, leaving the two adults for Quentin to work with. Fortunately, one of the families adopting the babies was quite well informed as to their mating habits and offered to help with the process. This part of the experiments was way outside Quentin's comfort zone so he was glad for the help and much relieved. Months would pass before there would be a generation of genetically-modified lizards running around. This would probably not be well received by anyone and so all were solemnly sworn to secrecy in the matter.

Quentin didn't even tell Ann about this one but it troubled him. Did this count as 'keeping secrets from each other'? Yes, most definitely. Had he already kept plenty of secrets from her? Yes, he had. But they had agreed to not keep secrets in the future. He imagined how he might introduce the subject... "You know those stories about alligators in the sewer? Well, you just won't believe what we found..."

Eventually, Ann did hear all about the lizards, after Quentin had rambled on about them for half an hour, tossing out names and behaviors that couldn't possibly be that of humans in the workplace, laboratory, or anywhere else for that matter. Quentin was more than able to carry on a conversation, if it stuck to certain topics and completely avoided others. Ann was more than used to it by this time.

Chapter 15. The Concert

A concert was coming to Carnegie Hall, featuring the works of several new composers, but more importantly, one of the percussionists had been a high school classmate. Ann mentioned it three times at lunch that day before Quentin finally got the hint that he was supposed to ask her to accompany him to this event. It would be a date. A real date, not just a cup of coffee or a cannoli, but an actual *date* date—their second *official* date. Their relationship was moving so very fast... or at a glacial speed, depending on which you asked.

The night arrived and Quentin was a basket case, fussing over his attire. He watched three videos before attempting to lash the noose (that is, bowtie) around his neck. He had decided to purchase the tuxedo rather than simply rent it, terrified that he might spill food on it, though they had no plans to eat that evening—at least together. He couldn't possibly eat under this stress, though she probably would.

He picked her up and they were on the way before a new wave of panic hit him: how far was the parking from where they would go in and were there stairs or an elevator or some other obstacle? He mumbled a few of these concerns before Ann suggested, "Just pull up out front and let them park it."

"Why would they do that?"

"It's called *valet* parking."

"Oh, yes, I forgot about that."

"Just calm down," she soothed. "This will be a delightful evening. No stress."

The parking attendant was much relieved to see that Ravi was going in and not staying in the car. As they approached the entrance Quentin blurted, "Where do we purchase the tickets?"

A man standing nearby looked down his nose in disgust. "This isn't the movies. This concert was sold out weeks ago."

"Don't worry," Ann chimed in. "I got two free tickets from the Station. We're good. Thank you."

The man sneered and moved away. When they got up to the door, another man in a uniform that looked like a waiter on the Titanic held up his hand. "No way! You're not coming in here with that thing!" He commanded, pointing at Ravi.

"But I'm blind," Ann replied.

"I don't care if you're deaf," the man shot back.

"That would be stupid," Quentin muttered. "Coming to a concert, I mean."

"He's perfectly safe," Ann insisted.

"He's a lot smarter than you," Quentin added, which only increased the man's obstinance.

They appeared to be at an impasse, until a voice broke into their predicament. "They're with me. Step aside!" It was the smartly-dressed woman from the sidewalk encounter with Animal Control. A tiger didn't rattle this jerk but a stare from that woman did, for he stepped aside and swept them into the Hall.

Ann recognized the voice and said, "Thank you again. I never caught your name the first time you rescued me from some bonehead."

"Beth Harper, Deputy Director of Homeland Security."

"Glad you came along when you did or we might have missed the Concert."

As they passed through the foyer Beth looked at Ravi, then over to Quentin and remarked, "If you're serious about working with gators, I can get you a mama and papa."

"No one is supposed to know about that," Quentin mumbled nervously, eyes darting back-and-forth.

"At Homeland we know everything that's going on."

"Oh, I guess so..."

"If you could teach them to play football, that would be huge—a full ride scholarship for sure."

"I don't think the NCAA would like that," Quentin squeaked.

"It's a joke," Beth replied. "Lighten up. Enjoy the music."

They did and it was excellent. Quentin and Ann were a little concerned that Ravi would be upset by the volume but he swayed and nodded his head to the music and, if anything, got more out of it than they did. The Director of Homeland was off to her own business but after the Concert the Percussionist brought the Conductor over to meet Quentin, Ann, and especially Ravi. Much to Quentin's chagrin, the story of their meeting and being sat upon was retold. Ann didn't seem to mind and so he eased up a bit.

Eventually, they were back in the car and headed off. They hadn't discussed anything after the Concert. Quentin wasn't the type to have a favorite pub for a nightcap and so now he struggled with what to do next. Should he suggest they stop somewhere and get a... what? Drink? That didn't seem right. A meal? Of course not. A cup of coffee? Certainly not.

He didn't actually make a decision on this and the ride was quiet. Somehow they were back in front of Ann's apartment, though he wasn't exactly sure how they got there. His lips moved but no sound came out. Presently she spoke. "And where are we?"

"Outside your apartment."

"Then you're taking me home?"

"Yes, of course, home... *your* home, that is," he stuttered. "I would never take you back to *my* place. That would be so presumptuous. I would never, ever, presume you would like spend the night and you know..."

"It's OK," Ann said reassuringly. "We've had a delightful evening. Let's not spoil it now."

"No, no, of course not... no spoiling... delightful evening... positively delightful in every single possible way imaginable... wonderful music, I mean... and being there with you, of course. That's the best part. You are sweeter than any music. I shouldn't say that. You are sweet... so very sweet... and patient with me..."

Before Quentin melted into a puddle, she reached out and touched his shoulder. He stopped talking and relished the moment. She opened the door, Ravi squeezed between them and out after her. The awkward moment had passed. He walked with her up to the door. She opened it as before and waited. This time he briefly kissed her waiting lips. Briefly, as in millisecond movement that would put the Flash to shame. She smiled and accepted the next tiny notch forward in their relationship.

* * *

Quentin verbally beat himself senseless as he drove away into the night. At last he forced his mind to travel elsewhere... What about alligators? Could they work like service dogs too? Could they waddle around the streets of New York City and ride the Subway. The very thought of it was hilarious. He couldn't get the idea of them playing football out of his head and so he drifted off to dreamland imagining eleven alligators chasing eleven razorbacks around a football field with fans cheering.

The next morning Quentin was in the Laboratory organizing notes and considering what to try next. He filled the little dish with Meow Mix that sat in the cage of the only surviving Iguana baby. He couldn't help but feel sorry for this little fellow, who had no one to play with. As he watched, the lizard pushed the pieces of food this way and that. After several minutes it became obvious he was sorting them by color or flavor or whatever, for there were three distinct kinds of kibbles. After sorting, he ate each pile in turn.

"You don't like your carrots to touch your peas," Quentin observed. "I wonder where you got that from?"

The little guy looked up as if to say, "Duh! Daddy-O."

"You need a name," Quentin announced. "I shall call you Ignatius, Iggy for short. Not Saint Ignatius of Loyola but the very philosophical Ignatius of Antioch. I think that suits you just fine."

Iggy then sorted a bag of M&M's but did not eat any of them. "You have a selective palette, I see."

Iggy spent the next two hours exploring Quentin's desk, which was piled with papers. "Now for the big test," Quentin announced, took a jar lid, scooped up the little pile of poo from Iggy's cage with it, and sat it in the middle of the desk. "Let's see if we can litter box train you and dispense with the cage."

Chapter 16. The Parents

"The time has come to meet the parents," Ann said during their evening phone call, which had recently become a daily thing.

"Which parents?" Quentin inquired nervously.

"First, you come over and meet mine. Dinner will, of course, be served. Then I will come over and meet yours."

"Can we do that?"

"Of course, it's the next logical thing."

"Next what? Logical how?"

"When two people are in a relationship they get to know each other's family."

"Are we in a re... relat... relationship?"

"Yes, of course. We've been on at least two *real* dates plus several not-by-chance meetings at Starbucks plus I sat on you in high school."

"I'm so very sorry about that," Quentin whimpered.

"I'm not," Ann laughed. "We wouldn't be having this conversation or in this *relationship* if I hadn't."

Quentin took a deep breath and said, "Then I'm glad you did too." And so their relationship notched up just a little bit more.

* * *

The date and time were set. Quentin picked Ann up at her apartment at precisely six that evening and they began the drive to Brooklyn Heights, where Ann's parents lived in a brownstone. Surprisingly, there was a parking spot not too far away and so they were soon at the door making introductions.

"This is Quentin. This is my mom, Margaret, and my dad, Dennis."

"Please do come in," Mom said. "Dinner will be ready soon and we can have a little sit and get acquainted."

Quentin sat nervously, expecting to be grilled like the guilty on the witness stand in the movies but it wasn't nearly so.

All sat but Mom, who asked, "Can I get anyone a glass of wine or some tea?"

"Just tea for me," Quentin said. "I'm driving."

"Please top mine off," Dad said.

Mom returned with two glasses of tea, one for Quentin and one for Ann, then filled Dad's glass, who began... "Tell us about your research."

Quentin took a deep breath and began... "I always wanted to do something in genetics and also the environment. At first, I didn't know how the two might overlap but this guy came and spoke, Dr. Booth, and that got it started. We totally stumbled across the tiger embryos. I've had some success with sewer rats and more recently an Iguana. He's just so cute! I have him potty trained and everything. He does tricks too. I swear he'll do anything for an apple."

Quentin rambled on about the research throughout the evening. "Do you watch Wheel of Fortune?" he asked at one point.

"Not really," Mom replied.

"Not if I can help it," Dad added.

"Then you'd love Gen-TV! They will watch *anything but* Wheel of Fortune. Gen-CP, the couch potatoes, can't stay awake that long."

"These are lizards?"

"No, no they're sewer rats. It's not that Gen-CP is all that stupid. They're just totally lazy. Pretty much all they do is eat and beg for more food."

"I don't think I've ever actually seen a sewer rat," Mom admitted.

"They look like regular rats, only furrier and bigger, about the size of a cat... a large cat. Of course, my guys would scare the fur off a cat. I guess that's why you never hear about cats in the sewer."

"So these rats are more intelligent?" Dad inquired suspiciously. "Isn't that the making of a Michael Crichton movie, which are all about people doing things that should never be done?"

"Oh, we've had the talk about that one," Quentin said reassuringly. "They know not to sneak off to NIMH or take over the world."

"Nimh?" Mom puzzled.

"National Institute of Mental Health," Quentin explained. "It's a story about Mrs. Frisby and some experimental rats that escaped and set up home in the wild."

"You had the *talk* with who?" Dad asked.

"The guys... I mean the *rats* and trust me, they know this is serious and not a game."

"You had the *talk* with the *rats*?"

"Oh, they love stories. I read to them and they curl up and listen, even the couch potatoes. They can stay awake for a while if it's a really good story. They just love Cat and the Hat and the Jungle Book."

Eventually, Mom said, "Oh, look at the time. You best be off. I'm sure you both have plans for tomorrow."

On the doorstep Quentin kissed Ann on the lips for nearly a full second before dashing off to the car.

* * *

One week later, it was time for Ann to meet Quentin's parents, who lived on Staten Island. He felt a little more comfortable, what with it being his family and having survived the ordeal of the previous week with nary a broken bone or missing limb.

Quentin was a little more formal. "Ann, this is my mother, Jamie, and my father, Bill. Er... um... I mean, Mom, this is Ann. Dad, this is also Ann. I mean... Also Dad, this is Ann too... also. And, of course, you already know Ravi."

"Yes, we know," Jamie said. "We've heard so much about you. It's so good to finally meet you."

"Quentin is so very fond," Bill started. "I mean... he speaks of you often. Not too often, of course, just from time-to-time. On occasion, really... yes, more often than not but not too often, of course... never too often."

"Please come in," Jamie said, directing them into the living room.

"We now know where the nervous behavior genes came from," Ann thought to herself.

"Come tell us what you've been doing since high school," Jamie started the conversation.

"I have always listened to the radio and audio books," Ann began. "They have meant so much to me and allowed me to travel to far away places, at least in my mind. And so I have always dreamed of a career in broadcasting. I got a two-year degree and then a certificate. A job became available at my favorite radio station, WNYG, and I really connected with the staff. Before long I was on the air, with my own show. It's not just me. Tonya and I work it together plus the two technicians. We couldn't possibly pull it off without them. It really does take a team and I'm so blessed to be part of a team doing something I love. I know not everyone has that... ever."

"That's great!" Jamie interjected.

"Our programming is always upbeat and encouraging. We have people calling in almost every day with stories of how we have inspired them or played the song they really needed to hear in the moment. I don't want people to think of me as being handicapped. Many people who tune in don't know, at least, I don't think they know. They do say things like, 'Did you see this or that,' so I guess they don't realize I'm blind."

The dinner was great and Ann commented several times, thinking the Grandmother had passed along some amazing recipes and skills. The evening was a little less awkward and that meant net progress in the right direction. They did talk some in the car on the way back to Ann's apartment, which was also encouraging. This relationship just might blossom into the real thing after all.

On the porch the pause before making contact was a little shorter and the lip contact was a little longer plus there was a tiny aftershock, peck on the cheek before Quentin scampered off to the car. There was a difference in his step, which Ann could hear... another notch.

Chapter 17. The Award

Professor Croft had been on the faculty for thirty-seven years. Just this past semester he had finally achieved deity, that is, tenure. This unusually long period of pre-tenure in preparation for the ascension did not escape his notice. It wasn't for lack of effort or even for lack of publications, albeit these essentially consisted of 256 possible arrangements of the same six words. You see, in order to attain a throne, one must be recommended for that pedestal and Croft was not one to engender support. In fact, most of the faculty and students avoided him whenever possible. The life-long sworn nemeses who held Croft back all these years had died off or finally retired. The remaining newer ones might not be able to succinctly relate what all the fuss was about, but could easily condense down to, "He's just so obnoxious."

If ever there was a prize on which Croft set his heart beyond tenure, it was the Annual Award for Excellence in Research, conferred by Frontiers in Genetics, the magazine published by the International Coalition for Genetic Research. When news broke that the exceedingly insignificant and spectacularly unworthy Quentin Farley was this year's recipient and to be honored at a star speckled banquet of celebrities in the field of genetic research, Croft exploded into random molecules—well, almost. He did clutch his chest and collapse to the floor in the weekly staff meeting.

After several rounds of, "Don't look at me!" "I don't know CPR." "I can do it, but not on *him!*" Someone mumbled, "The kiss of life... or death, as the case may be." Booth bent over the twitching body of Croft and pronounced him to be very much alive. The whispers of, "too bad," were barely audible. Professor Croft did survive and when sufficiently recovered, broke forth in a tirade worthy of Napoleon Bonaparte, casting blame on others for losing the Battle of Waterloo. Croft may have dismissed Quentin before, but now he despised the little sewer rat and vowed to destroy him.

* * *

Professor Croft's long and noteworthy career in genetic research began with a tiny single-celled organism named Escherichia coli, or E. coli for short. This particular strain was no ordinary ameba, no mere amorphous blob of protoplasm. This dreaded killer, thought to have slain thousands in 1846 and again in 1864, filling every available bed in legendary Bellevue Hospital, came from the steamy depths of the netherworld that lies beneath the sprawling city of New York. No organized crime boss could possibly claim the casualties of this Scourge of the Sewer, this Denizen of the Dump, this Blight of the Bowery, this

Curse of the Culverts, this Plague of the Pipes. This tiny Master of Massacre, borne on the Wings of Waste, is literally what you spread around when you don't wash your hands after pooping, so you can find it just about anywhere; but it does sound so much more important if you use the Latin name and throw in some nifty adjectives.

Over the past thirty-seven years, Professor Croft had served as midwife to more than sixty thousand generations of E. coli. Those honored progenitors of this vast horde upon horde of heartless killers had him to thank for their existence. Of course, they would have done just fine in the Sewer. Still, the Professor dutifully fed and nurtured each and every one. He separated them into countless colonies, feeding each one on practically every item available at the grocery store. Always taking careful note as to the impact on their health and number.

Croft had, from first entering graduate school, recorded their genes to meticulous detail upon detail, tirelessly logging and mapping each generation and colony, naming them in order and gathering the information into a voluminous database. He even drew an eight-foot-tall family tree of these his precious flock. Of course, the tree only had one branch and after all this ridiculous fuss, instead of sheep, these were all still E. coli, albeit of the genus New Yorkus Toxicus Rex, a designation he was never able to get properly recognized by the scientific community. Oh, well... their loss.

* * *

How could these morons at the Coalition hand this cherished Award to some kid was beyond Croft's comprehension. This lofty honor had only twice been bestowed on anyone less than a seated faculty and those were post-doctoral candidates, hardly the same category as Quentin. Still, he should have seen this coming. He was the only one to object when Quentin was put forward for candidacy into graduate school. He had objected again after the master's when the doctorate had been floated in the weekly staff meeting. Had it not been for Booth, the Buffoon, this would never have happened. It was that money from DOD that cinched the deal. Money... It's always about the money and never about the science. Booth and his Pentagon money had bought Quentin's degree and was now buying him this cherished honor.

After the meeting in which Croft crumpled to the floor, Booth went straight to Quentin's Laboratory and said, "You must wrap this up now. Type 'The End' and push 'Print'. I will schedule your defense and we will move on to the next phase. If Croft can get any traction—which he no doubt will—and get anyone else behind him on this, you're toast and so is our Project here."

* * *

Two weeks later, the dissertation was done and the oral defense was scheduled. Professor Croft was fuming mad, but hadn't built a coalition, at least not yet as far as Booth could ascertain. Quentin prepared a series of slides for

PowerPoint along with an outline tucked up his sleeve. He was in the conference room setting up before any of the faculty arrived. Iggy rode up from the basement on Quentin's shoulder and now sat on top of the mouse beside the laptop, poised to assist.

The faculty straggled in, including Croft and Booth. The presentation began with some basics, then dove straight into the intricate details of the chemicals, molecules, and how it all came together. There were fifty-four slides, some featuring multiple graphs. Quentin explained them all with surprising confidence, perhaps due to having his little buddy there showing support. After describing the details, Quentin would say, "Next slide please," and Iggy would tap the mouse with his chin. Each time this happened, Croft let out a little sputter of disgust, followed by a glare. These hostile reactions continued throughout the presentation, slowly edging upward in aggression. Other faculty asked questions but not Croft, as he was saving his verbal assault until the end.

Six of the twelve members of the Faculty had read the dissertation and were just waiting to sign it. They had digested the material and were duly impressed by the depth and quality. They asked a few questions, none too difficult and certainly not confrontational. The half who were a little less familiar were surprised to discover what had been developing under their feet—literally down in the basement Laboratory. They were quite pleased, knowing that the reputation of the Department and they themselves would benefit from the work. Twice Croft started to interject a comment, but someone beat him to it—a graph here, a symbol there, a note too small to read elsewhere.

Surprisingly, there was little discussion of the tigers and the daughter of the President. There was also little mention of the Pentagon connection and the source of funding. There were a few questions about the origin of the organisms and chemicals. Booth had coached Quentin in these particulars, so that they were simply designated Site 1, 2, 3, etc. and Sample 4, 5, 6, etc. Quentin was much relieved that no one pulled the fire alarm or blurted out, "Did this stuff come from an Iranian bio-weapons lab and you brought it into this very building?"

There were several questions about the wisdom of meddling in genetics and the possible apocalyptic consequences if the smarter batch of sewer rats decided to elope with Mrs. Frisby, though they didn't phrase it that way, simply suggesting they might sneak out and head back to the sewer. Quentin handled these questions well too, as Booth had coached and they had practiced time and again.

Only three slides to go... only two slides... on the last slide now... just a few more comments and wrap it up...

At last it was over and Quentin had survived... at least it looked that way to him and Booth, but Croft had a different plan. "This is preposterous!" the indignant offended professor bellowed. "It's pure rubbish—a complete fabrication. Anyone could train a tiger born in captivity. That doesn't prove a blasted thing!" At this point Croft came up out of his chair and lunged forward toward the table supporting the laptop. "This stupid leggo robot rubber lizard thing is an insult to our intelligence!" With this said, he swung his arm out to bat said *thing* from the table, but this was no rubber lizard! Iggy pushed up to his full height, arched his back, extended his spiked fins, and hissed with surprising menace. Croft's eyes fairly popped out of his head. He quickly drew back his hand and rolled over two chairs, taking them to the floor with him. Croft flopped about on the floor, kicking and cursing.

Booth rolled his eyes and moaned, "Here we go again."

Quentin rushed to Iggy, stroked him softly and murmured, "It's OK, Little Buddy. The mean old man isn't going to hurt me."

After repeatedly insisting, "I'm fine! Leave me alone!" Two EMTs arrived and put Croft on a stretcher. He refused to be taken to the Hospital but the Department Chairman said, "Sorry... It's policy—especially after the last time you collapsed."

Chapter 18. The Job

Croft was not there to object when the nods were given, signaling that Quentin was now Dr. Farley, or at least would soon be following the ceremony. The Dissertation was signed and submitted to the Graduate School, whose part in all this was still a complete mystery. The Graduation Fee was duly paid—for what we will never know... the paper and cardboard tube perhaps? The cap and gown were retrieved from deep within the closet, vigorously shaken out, and looked good enough to wear again. No need for dry-cleaning. Booth and the Folks were there to cheer and so were Ann and Ravi. Iggy was disappointed not to be there but neither Mom nor Dad would agree to let him ride in on their shoulder, presuming they would let a very intelligent actual lizard in the building. They all went out to 7-7-6 for dinner, where Quentin received more congratulations.

Strange as it might seem, he had never given much thought to being at this point in life and what might come next. Dad mentioned it about half-way through the meal and Booth said, "I was hoping Quentin would come work for me. We still have lots to do and I'd hate to have to break in a new cowpoke at this stage of the cattle drive." That got a laugh and they moved on. Could it possibly be that simple? Pack up the stuff in the Lab and go to work at CleanWater, Inc.? They didn't have a local facility. Booth had the little office on campus plus a few things in his basement. All the lab work before arranging things at the University was done in their Arlington branch, which Quentin had visited several times, but was much too far for a daily commute.

Oh, boy! The obvious just slapped him across the face... If he moved pretty much anywhere, it would be farther away from Ann and would decrease their time together. Could he rent an apartment closer to her and fill it with lab equipment? That would never work. The cultures, three generations of sewer rats, half of which were pregnant! His mind was spinning. Iggy's parents went to a pet store, where they found new homes, but he had *promised* the little guy a girlfriend soon. He couldn't go back on his word. If Iggy and Izzy got together, soon there would be iguanalets and he just *had* to find out what would happen in the second generation. If they were all as smart as their Papa, he would have to home school them.

Quentin began to squirm and sweat, juggling all the complexities and possibilities in his mind. He was the only one not eating by this point and the others were beginning to show some concern. Then out of the blue Booth said, "The Company has just bought a little place on Staten Island. It was a commercial bakery for seventy-five years but has been abandoned—one of too many businesses who closed their doors with COVID and never recovered. We're going to set up shop there. Plenty of room and very convenient, within walking distance of where the Ferry lands. It's perfect."

Wow! That fast... the panic came and then it went... Iggy would soon be alone no more. Ouch! He couldn't just buy a female at a pet shop and bring her home. This wasn't like grocery shopping or getting a new car. This would require planning and options. How many iguanas were there in the New York area? Could he get them all to submit photos? Of course there's no dating site for iguanas... or is there? He hadn't checked. Must do that soon.

Quentin had resumed shoveling food by this time. He looked past the fork of pasta and locked eyes on Ann. Ahh... the princess of his dreams. Hard to believe she was sitting right across the table. Hard to believe he had gotten to this point. Hard to believe he had finished school—at last. Hard to believe he had a job. Hard to believe he was ready for the next phase of life. With school in the rear view mirror, he must now concentrate—or at least focus his thoughts— on Ann and their *relationship*. Yikes! He was an adult and seriously considering a relationship with a *woman*. How did this happen?

* * *

It took a week to move everything out of the Lab at University and into the Bakery on Staten Island. Iggy had been living in the apartment and riding around in the car long before this. The sewer rats were pleased with the new accommodations, especially Gen-CP, who he suspected were quite aware of what had been the function of this place for decades. He could almost hear them demanding, "Like when will the loaves be ready to eat?" "I don't know about youze guyze, but I could go for a loaf right about now." "Yeah, me toose. It's gotta be suppertime somewhere."

Perhaps it was best that they couldn't talk. Quentin couldn't get the imagined voices out of his head. His dreams—when they weren't of Ann—were filled with New York sewer rat conversations...

"You take the gun and leave me the cannoli."
"Who needs a gun when ya got a cannoli?"
"Who cares about da ponies? All I cares about is da cannoli."
"So, make me a stromboli I can't refuse."
"Go ahead and make my day, only make it with oregano this time!"

While Quentin was discussing the lack of a dating app for iguanas with the pet store clerk, Iggy was straddling the cash register and minding business. A woman came in with an ailing iguana that had some sort of a skin rash. When Quentin looked over, Iggy was completely limp, with tongue hanging out and eyes bulging. Quentin panicked, fearing someone had hit the little guy, thinking he had escaped from a cage; but it soon became clear that Iggy was love-struck. The sickly iguana turned out to be female and was not opposed to Iggy's overtures. Quentin and the Woman exchanged phone numbers and promised to plan a date very soon, when the salve had done its work and the rash cleared.

* * *

Quentin and Booth had never even discussed salary. After two weeks when the deposit showed up in his bank account, Quentin was shocked. "I guess Mom and Dad are off the hook now. I could actually have some choice in where to live..." But this created a new dilemma...

Move to Staten Island, closer to the Lab. No... wait... Move closer to the Radio Station or to Ann's Apartment. Get a place where we could live together? Like in twenty or thirty years maybe? Sooner maybe? Would that be possible? How long is the standard waiting period? I mean... the engagement or whatever you call it.

This conversation was inside Quentin's mind but Iggy was staring at him with deepening concern from atop the computer monitor. He could almost hear Iggy say, "Marriage? Engagement? You haven't popped the question yet. You haven't even properly kissed her yet. Even I understand these things better than you. My relationship with Izzy is progressing on schedule while yours with Ann is stuck in the mud. Our kids will be off to college before you get to second base."

Quentin gasped and blinked. "Have you done the... you know... with Izzy? Is she... preg... like with lizardlets?"

"Quentin, my man, you are so clueless," Iggy conveyed with a sigh—not verbally, of course. If only the lizard could talk. "Of course not. These things take time and a certain finesse. You know, take it slow and steady. Not your kind of slow, which is glacial, but learn to read the cues. She will let you know when she's ready."

"Queues? Like waiting in a line," Quentin mumbled.

"No, Bro, not queues, *cues* like move closer, you can kiss me now."

"They do that?"

"Yes, except with us it's all in the neck... see..." Iggy puffed out his throat.

"But she's blind. How will she know when I puff out my throat?"

Iggy repositioned himself as if to get more comfortable and prepare for a very long lecture on the birds and the bees, or in this case, the lizards and the humans. The two stared at each other for quite some time before Quentin realized what time it was and that he had arranged to meet Ann at the coffee shop. He took the bridge, parked in the more expensive but closer garage, and dashed the last four blocks to the Café, where Ann sat having a conversation with Ravi, which, as you might expect was about how clueless Quentin was and how they might best prod him forward.

71

They sipped coffee and talked of things... lots of things, but not so much about their relationship. Quentin had an idea to invite Ann to see the fireworks at Battery Park that evening, but just as he was winding up to deliver the invitation it hit him... Explosions in the air that you can't see would be very upsetting for a blind person and a really stupid suggestion for a date. Perhaps the latest Ghostbusters movie? No, clueless, what a stupid idea. A Broadway play perhaps? Maybe... if it had a lot of singing. How about an opera? For the rest of their time before Ann had to scurry back to the Station, Quentin imagined Elmer Fudd singing, "To kill the wabbit... To kill the wabbit..."

Chapter 19. The Ferry

When traveling back-and-forth between the City and Staten Island, some times Quentin took the Verrazzano Bridge and other times he took the Ferry. The Ferry quit transporting cars after 9/11 but he could park near the Dock on either side and easily walk from the Ferry to the Lab on South end of this route. His folks place was on the opposite side of the Island. On one of those trips, while standing near the bow of the ship, the idea hit him...

"I have a surprise for you," he began the conversation.

"This sounds interesting," she smiled.

"An adventure, really..." he explained.

"Climbing Everest?" she asked teasingly.

"Not quite so high."

"The Empire State Building?"

"A little lower, closer to the water."

"OK... When?"

"I was thinking of this evening."

"I must consult my calendar... Let me see... Addressing the United Nations... Meeting with the President and Joint Chiefs of Staff... Solving world hunger... OK, I can squeeze you in this evening."

"How about I pick you up at the Station."

"Sounds like a plan."

* * *

"So... where are we going?" Ann inquired.

"That's a surprise... remember," Quentin deflected.

They drove South to the waterfront and parked. As they stepped onto the Ferry, Ann could feel the difference. "Are you taking me on a cruise?"

"Yes... but not exactly a Disney cruise with Mickey and Minnie and Pluto and all that."

Eventually, the crew cast off and the ship got under weigh. Quentin led Ann with Ravi out to the bow. The forward motion along with a little breeze was just enough to provide the feel he had hoped for. "Lean into the wind," he urged, nodding to Ravi, who also got into the mood. Then Quentin took out his phone, pushed the volume up all the way, and tapped the YouTube app, which filled the space with the theme to Titanic.

Ann smiled and breathed in, not only the feeling of budding love from the Movie but also the relief that Quentin had finally done something romantic. It was happening, even if at a snail's pace, still their relationship was moving forward. When they reached the other side, Quentin moved to stand beside Ann and put his arm around her shoulder. She laid her head against his side and relished the moment.

On the return voyage, Quentin actually kissed Ann... twice! Good so far... as long as we don't hit an iceberg, of course. But this was not to be a remake of the movie in several ways, for at that moment a flock of squealing kids rushed up to meet Ravi. It seems a class of fourth-graders had been on a field trip and were onboard. More than half of them were excited to pet a real tiger, but a few held back with the Teacher for reassurance.

When they were back in the car and before driving to Luigi's for dinner—also a surprise—Ann remarked, "That was fun. We could do it again some time."

"Yes, we must," Quentin replied, surprised at his own reaction to this new element of their merging paths. He still could hardly believe that he was this close—in the same car even—to her... the love of his life. As they coursed the busy streets of the City, he thought back to their past...

* * *

One day in the school lunchroom, Quentin spied Ann sitting alone at a table eating. The room was somewhat filled, but not so much as it often was. Many of the students were off on a field trip to Washington plus others were out sick, for a bout of the flu was making the rounds. He slid in opposite her and inquired nervously, "Is this seat taken?"

"I guess not," she replied with a chuckle, "as you're already sitting in it."

In spite of being blind, she picked up on lots of things from sound alone. She was very smart that way... and other ways too, often raising her hand in class to answer questions, even when nobody else was. Beautiful and smart too... Wow! What a combination. She was *way* out of his league—mister nerd face... the Dork... the Loser... Have to sneak up on a clock to see the time of day according to one bully that even looked like Scut Farkus. One kiss from him would turn any princess into a toad according to an actual Mean Girl who could be Regina George's doppelganger.

He was sulking, wallowing in self-pity, unable to speak when she broke the silence between then. "So... you've just moved here from where exactly?"

"We moved here from Chandler, which is near Asheville, North Carolina. It's a small town with a lot of woods and open spaces—nothing like New York City," he replied.

"So why did you move here?"

"My dad works for Dander-Murphy, a wholesale office supply company. He did very well in sales so when a spot came open in the main branch here, they offered him the job and he pounced on it."

"Is the Boss named Michael?"

"No, it's Bruce something."

"But is the Secretary named Pam?"

"I don't really know. Dad doesn't talk about the Office that much."

"How about Dwight or Kevin or Jim?" Ann was laughing so hard by this time that she was dribbling food.

"Dad talks about a guy named Glen that works in the warehouse," Quentin stammered.

"Of course he does!" Ann exclaimed. "Plus Phillip and Lonny and..."

Quentin was blinking and twitching and mumbling by this point, as Ann guffawed while applying the paper napkin. "The *Office*..."

"Yes," Quentin fairly squeaked. "Dad works at the office some days but not every day. Some days he's on the road making sales calls."

"Not the office," Ann chuckled. "*The Office*."

"Yes, the office. It's an office. In a building."

"The Office on TV."

"I don't think they have a television set in Dad's office."

"The television show... The Office... You know... Steve Carell as Michael Scott, Jenna Fischer as Pam Beesly, John Krasinski as Jim Halpert, and Rainn Wilson as Dwight Schrute?"

"Oh... yes... *that* office..."

"Dander-Murphy... Dunder-Mifflin... I bet they get prank calls all the time."

"Prank calls? Yeah, sure... all the time..." Quentin was in a death spiral at this point...

Well, I sure blew that one.
Had my big chance... stuck my foot in it.
Now she thinks I'm a complete moron.
Just dump my lunch in the trashcan and dive in with it.

Ann sensed that what should have been fun and banter had not turned out well...

I'm pretty sure he likes me but...
We can't even have a normal fun conversation...
Is it just me? Is it because I'm blind?
How could I have handled this differently?
Should I say something? Should I apologize?

75

I haven't done anything wrong.
It's not like I was making fun of his Dad or the business.
It was just a laugh...

Chapter 20. The Pub

That evening Ann and Tonya met nine others from the Station at the Big Apple Pub for drinks, dancing, and entertainment. A special group named Lonely No More was performing that night. They had one hit song of their own, by the same name, plus they performed others from similar groups of the same genre. They performed their hit three times, at nine, ten, and eleven. It was good and no one complained of the repetition. The lead vocalist had a remarkable voice and did a masterful job with *My Heart Will Go On*, the theme song from *Titanic*. This turned Ann's thoughts back to the Ferry and Quentin, which was a little bit of a downer for her.

Ann—always super careful about imbibing anything risky—nursed a single glass of the house white wine throughout the evening. Ravi lapped a dish of water and nibbled on a few of the appetizers but was not impressed with the food. He ate one buffalo chicken wing but declined a second. Overall, the evening was not much of a party for either of them. Ravi did sway with the Titanic, making Ann think he was recalling their time on the bow of the Ferry, but sat stone still for most of the evening.

A rather loud and obviously intoxicated woman at a nearby table took an interest in Ravi, blowing lip-smacking kisses, calling him Puddy Tat. After the fourth or fifth time of this Ann mumbled, "tiger," but the woman apparently didn't hear. Eventually, she leaned over and enunciated, "He is a Bengal tiger and his name is Ravi."

This got a response... The woman stumbled over and said, "I used to date a guy named Ravi. He was a computer geek and like a super programmer that all the companies were after to create games or movies or something. A complete and total nerd but like drop-dead handsome."

"I kinda know what you mean," Ann admitted.

"He would like never make the *move*... you know... the *big* move... I sat on his lap once and he about wet himself."

"I know *exactly* what you mean," Ann chuckled.

"So, he took me home to meet his parents. Apparently, that's a thing they do in India. Nothing like the movie with Ben Stiller and Robert De Niro, of course. It turns out that everyone else in the family is a doctor—a *real* doctor who operates on people, he tells me, not a *pretend* doctor who lectures at Uni, like him."

"Still with you," Ann agreed.

"They take one look at me and puke. Grandma clutches her chest and collapses on the floor. I guess it's a good thing to be in a house full of doctors, cause soon they have her sitting on the couch taking deep breaths. One of them whips out a stethoscope while another takes her pulse. It was just like an episode of General Hospital. The rest of them are gaping at me with their mouths hanging open. I'm surprised some pigeons didn't build a nest in there."

"One sister points at my arm like it's a cobra and asks, 'Is that per... perm... permanent?' 'You mean the tat?' I ask. She nods her head. I say, 'Of course, and so is this!' and pull up my blouse to show the dolphins on my stomach. I mean, who doesn't like dolphins? The other sister collapses on the couch next to Granny and the mom starts muttering in some strange language like she's speaking in tongues—not that I've ever been to a church that passes out snakes, of course, but my cousin grew up in one and I've heard all the stories. I think Mom is trying to exorcize my demons, which must be legion from the way she's moaning and calling out."

"Then Grandpa comes to assist, which is some sort of hand waving and I get the message that they're sweeping me out of the house and into the fires of perdition. The Dad hasn't moved since all this started. But this is really creepy... his eyes move independently—one on me the whole time and one on Ravi, who is horrified and frozen with indecision."

"I think it's about time to make my exit and say as much to Ravi. He follows me out because he has to drive me home unless I'm going to hitchhike a ride. We're in the car in complete silence for at least fifteen minutes before he says anything. 'Sorry.' 'That's it?' I ask. 'After that performance all you got to say is, 'sorry'.' He's on the verge of tears. 'I don't think this is going to work.' He finally mumbles. 'Ya think not?' I shoot back. 'I mean, us.' He adds. 'I got that part.'"

"How could he not see this coming?" she demanded.

"Guys can be pretty clueless," Ann replied.

"By the way, my name's Alice."

"Ann here and I appreciate your sharing the story. Not that I've been there but I can imagine and have an awkward guy in my life too."

"Seriously? Is he a computer geek as well?"

"No, he's into genetics. That's how I came to have Ravi, who is no ordinary tiger. He's really smart."

At this point a guy stepped up and said, "Alice! So nice to see you." He then spoke to Ann, "Can I save this damsel from the jaws of the tiger... with a martini perhaps?"

Ann said, "Sure," and the two moved away, chatting as they went. The night wore on and it was getting late, so Ann excused herself and left the Pub to begin the walk back to the subway and the other side of town. As they passed along the sidewalk and came to the opening, which was an alley between two buildings, lined with a few trashcans and several dumpsters. Ravi suddenly stopped and turned toward a muffled sound. Ann heard it too.

"No! Stop!" then the faint sound of scuffling. "I don't care what we did before. That was then and this is now." The voice was urgent.

This was Alice. Ann was sure and so was Ravi, who advanced with determination. The voices became louder as the distance between them shrank.

"I just need a little lovin'."

"I just need a little space!"

"It's not like this is your first time."

"Get your paws off me!" Alice pleaded.

Just then, the *real paws* arrived on the scene. Ravi let out a deep growl the likes of which Ann had never heard. The sound reverberated in the alley. Alice gasped and froze. The man pawing Alice dropped his pants, then stooped to pick them up, as his courage ran down his legs into his shoes. The terrified man shuffled around them and waddled into the darkness, holding his belt and leaving a little trail behind.

"That was close!" Alice exclaimed. "I am so glad you guys came along when you did. He is the same old creep, in spite of all the sweet talk and promises. I have the worst luck with guys. They're either way too slow or way too fast or out on bail or on the terrorist watch list."

"I have never been in your situation," Ann sighed. "But I have been helpless and mugged twice."

"That stinks," Alice replied. "It's a good thing you have this guy now," giving Ravi a big hug, which was answered by a big lick on the cheek.

"I shudder to think how vulnerable I was before him."

"Does he have a brother?"

"Yes, as a matter of fact. His name is Tavi and he guides for Darcy Bates, the President's daughter."

"Are you serious? That's amazing!"

"I bet half the women in New York would give their teeth to have a tiger by their side, especially on the street or in the Subway."

"I don't think we're ready for that quite yet," Ann explained. "Ravi and Tavi are super smart because they're genetically modified. Without that extra smarts, they might do more harm than good on the street."

"Genetically modified... like how?" Alice inquired nervously.

"It's part of a larger study being conducted by the Pentagon, so please don't talk about this to anyone. The guys are extremely careful and taking it step-by-step. They're not mixing DNA in the blender to see what comes out and they're not going to let dinosaurs escape to eat us all."

"That's a relief," Alice remarked. "The T-Rex in Jurassic Park was kinda cute but the Velociraptors give me the creeps."

"No dinosaurs as far as I know."

"Thanks again, Ravi, for saving me," Alice said, straightened her skirt and scurried off into the darkness of the City.

Chapter 21. The Escape

Quentin was watching each tiny vial, as it was shuttled along and through the analyzer, recording times and adding details to the spreadsheet for this latest batch of tests. The Bakery was a big improvement over the basement Lab at Uni. No rumbling random machines. No gurgling pipes. No interruptions and constant temperature. The ancient ventilation system at the School was almost random compared to the much newer one at the Bakery. Booth was bent over a microscope and scribbling on a pad, also intent on his work. The Pentagon was getting impatient and expecting progress and so there was much riding on this latest effort.

The phone rang and Booth answered in a dull voice. "Yes?"

Quentin continued with his samples, not paying attention.

When Booth fairly screamed into the phone, "Are you serious?" Quentin paused the analyzer and refocused his attention.

"You've got to be kidding? No way! You can't be serious! And how is this *our* problem? Owe them a favor? I already gave them my liver and both kidneys!"

Quentin looked over with growing concern at this distressing one-sided conversation. Booth put his other hand on the phone and spoke aside, "The poo has hit the fan!"

Booth let out a long sigh of resignation and disgust. "OK... OK... Calm down. We can fix this. I don't know how but we will do it. No, we can't let loose the tigers to gobble them up. I don't think they eat mice. Besides, we aren't going to risk them to fix someone else's problem."

Quentin turned the analyzer off, closed the spreadsheet, and put the lid down on the laptop. Whatever this was, it would take precedence.

"What exactly is the risk here? What do you mean, 'you can't say?' How bad could it be? COVID is already out and about. So it's *not* COVID, then what *is* it? Are we going to die? We've handled some really nasty stuff. Seriously? OK, how many are there? That's not too bad. Yes, I'm sure they can multiply but it doesn't happen over night? Thirty days is about average. OK, so we have a month to contain the problem."

At this point Booth jabbed the pencil into the pad, splintering it. "If you were going to dump this on us, then why didn't you call immediately. So then who did give the order? Oh... well... I guess we will do our best... See you soon..." click...

"So?" Quentin ventured.

"You're not going to believe this," Booth began. "Some idiot at the National Institute of Mental Health has been doing some sort of research on mice. We can't be trusted with knowing what or who. Apparently, a bumbling janitor knocked over a cage with six mice and they scampered off into the woodwork. No surprise there. We must find them before they turn into zombies and spread whatever it is that will make COVID seem like the common cold," Booth explained.

"Why don't they just fumigate the building and kill them off?" Quentin asked.

"Apparently, they already tried that partially, except that they can't possibly evacuate the building and empty it all out in time before the things breed and take over the world."

"Why don't they starve some cats and let them loose to chow down?"

"They already tried that and it didn't work. Apparently, we're on the final countdown to Mousemageddon."

"Why would they call *us* to take care of this mess?" Quentin puzzled.

"Guess..." Booth replied. "You're going to love this..."

"We're not the Ghostbusters. They know that, right?"

"Very funny and oh so close. Guess again..."

"They think our tigers are super cats and will swoop in to save the day?"

"Even closer..."

"Someone told them we had super powers?"

"Exactly!" Booth exclaimed. "The topic came up in a hush-hush meeting at the Whitehouse. Apparently, they think blind girls can't hear and treat them like wallpaper. She listens to the whole thing before interrupting to say, 'Just call Quentin. Problem solved...' and so they did, by way of the Pentagon and the Colonel, of course. She thinks if we solve this problem we'll be set life and can get eternal funding."

* * *

Six hours later, Booth and Quentin pulled up to the employee parking lot of NIMH in Bethesda, Maryland. The Guard at the gate stopped them for ID. Quentin rolled down the window and said, "We're the Ghostbusters."

"Very funny," the Guard shot back.

"*Mouse*busters," Booth clarified. "Dr. Price is expecting us."

This clarification clearly shook the Guard who said, "Yes, sure, park anywhere you like," and opened the gate.

The Guard must have called because a huddle of four people in white coats—two men and two women—scurried out of the building to meet them in the parking lot. Quentin and Booth got out of the van, each clutching two cat carriers. The spokesperson, presumably Dr. Price looked confused as he inquired, "We already tried cats. Where are the tigers?"

"No tigers," Booth explained. "Just sewer rats. Perfect for this job."

"Are you serious," the woman standing next to Price bellowed. "The rats have escaped from NIMH and you brought *more* rats? Do you think this is some kind of joke? These rodents are ticking time bombs, poised to spread the bubon—"

Price clapped his hand over the woman's mouth and interrupted. "The mice in question may possibly have come in contact with a pathogen of some concern—unintentionally, of course. Not that we do research on communicable diseases or anything like that, of course, you understand..." all the while vigorously shaking his head. The expression on the other's faces loudly proclaimed that the mice had indeed been injected with the plague or something worse and might spread it.

Booth motioned for them to turn and make for the building. "I'll explain as we go." The four complied, though reluctantly. "These are no *ordinary* sewer rats. They're intelligent and, most importantly, obedient."

"You're kidding, right?" Price balked.

The woman who spoke before asked, "Is one of them named Mrs. Frisby?"

"We call them Gen-TD," Quentin explained.

Booth interrupted before Quentin could say, "Tiny Dancers," which would, no doubt, blow the whole thing wide open. "They can count, which is essential, plus they can get into tight spaces. If you're not convinced. We'll leave."

The team from NIMH led the way to the building where the accidental release had occurred. They let out a simultaneous sigh of disgust and stood with hands on hips, expecting the worst from the Two Stooges, wondering when the Third Stooge would arrive.

Quentin and Booth opened the carriers and the four tiny dancers lined up like they were ready to perform the Swan Lake Ballet. Quentin motioned with his finger and the little furry ballerinas went through their routine. The four from NIMH were truly astonished. Could this possibly work? Quentin then pulled out his phone, brought up an image of a white mouse, and held up six fingers. Then he held the phone to his chest and patted it gently. Placing the phone on the floor, he put his hand to his forehead and looked about. Gen-TD watched these machinations with great interest. He then opened and closed his hands, splaying his fingers, and the Rat Team took off in separate directions, causing the NIMH Team to almost jump out of their shoes.

"Now what?" Dr. Price asked nervously.

"We wait," Booth replied.

Less than ten minutes later, one of the Rat Team returned to the room with two little white mice straggling along behind. The larger rat stopped, coaxed in some secret rodent language, arrived at Quentin's feet, and looked up with satisfaction.

"Well slap me silly and call me Sally," Dr. Price exclaimed. "I'm seeing it with my own eyes and I still don't believe it."

One of the Team went to fetch a cage and came back with a Lab Tech, who was clearly accustomed to handling the mice. A little treat to eat was offered and so the first two were present and accounted for. Over the next three hours, the Rat Team recovered eleven white mice. Six were of the same size, while five were noticeably larger. The woman, who had introduced herself as Dr. Kirk by this time, looked over at the Lab Tech and said, "Apparently, these six aren't the only ones out for a romp."

The tech guy took a step back and insisted, "It wasn't me. I swear."

"OK," Price interrupted. "Let's take DNA samples from them all and make absolutely sure we have the crucial six, plus figure out where these others got loose from. Every one is in the system, or at least they had better be or heads will roll."

Dr. Price turned to Quentin and Booth saying, "I can't believe you pulled this off or that I'm saying this, but thank you *so much* for averting a possible disaster of global proportion. If we discover there are more on the loose can we call you again?"

Quentin began and Booth finished, "When a mouse is *loose*... And about the *hoose*... Who you gunna call? *Mousebusters!*"

Chapter 22. The Cats

Quentin's mind was swirling with possibilities... all useless. Where do you take a blind girl on *the really big* special date? Movies? No. Fireworks? No. Ball game? No. Coney Island Amusement Park? No. Planetarium? No. Aquarium? No. The laboratory menagerie was staring at their human with increasing concern. Even the couch potatoes were sleepless and Iggy's throat was quivering. If only they could talk, the path forward was clear... at least to them, if not to him. Progress on the research had come to a grinding halt and Booth was off managing a clean up team in Oak Ridge, Tennessee, where the last remnants of the Manhattan Project were being loaded into trucks to be buried somewhere in Nevada which shall not be recorded or remembered.

Quentin stumbled over to the Ferry in hopes that the wind might blow an idea his way. It now had memories of her plus it was free. As it turned out, the Winds of Fate were blowing his way. A Passenger sat reading the Times—an actual physical newspaper. Quentin was a little surprised they still made the things, let alone that anyone actually bought one. Oh, yes, he had seen them many times on the Subway. That tidbit of information was stored in a little used neuron buried deep in the gray matter.

He could see the front page, which displayed the word 'Cats' in large bold letters. The Passenger turned a page, which slightly changed Quentin's view of the front, on which he now noticed the word 'Reunion'. "Cat reunion..." he thought, "sounds exciting... not!" This struck him as preposterous and so he looked closer. Just below the fold he saw the word, 'Paige', and thought, "I think they misspelled that one." He moved closer to discover this wasn't a type-o but a name, 'Elaine Paige'. Somewhere in deep recesses of his mind a song began to form...

Midnight, not a sound from the pavement.
Has the moon lost her memory?
She is smiling alone.
In the lamp light the whithered leaves collect at my feet,
and the wind, begins to moan.

By this time Quentin was sitting next to the Passenger, bent over his lap staring at the front page. The Man put down the paper and asked, "Would you like the front page? I've already read it."

"Yes... please," Quentin stammered. "I think my whole future depends on it."

It seems that the musical, *Cats*, featuring many of the original cast—most importantly—Elaine Paige, who propelled it to fame with her incomparable performance of the song, *Memories*, would appear once-and-only-once, this coming Friday night at the Winter Garden Theatre on Broadway. The heavens opened and thousands of cats burst forth in song—at least that's what it felt like in Quentin's head.

He called the Theater and after twenty minutes on hold, was informed that the Show had been sold out for weeks. The ground opened and devil cats moaned piteously over Quentin's hopeless predicament. Later that day, he dragged himself to the Café and sat for fifteen minutes before Tonya appeared and reminded him that Ann was in a meeting and couldn't make it. Concerned by his unusually downcast demeanor, she inquired as to the cause. He explained how miraculously the play of all plays, the greatest to ever grace a stage, Broadway or anywhere else, with many of the original cast, most importantly Elaine Paige, sprang into existence—the perfect destination for a date with Ann—just as miraculously vaporized, taking his hopes and dreams with it into Cata-gory and Purr-dition.

"Cheer up," she said with a pat on the shoulder. "We have a lot of very influential contacts and supporters of the Station. Somebody, somewhere must have two tickets to spare." Tonya made several calls and then enlisted the help of others in this cause to assist the all-important relationship, which was a continuous topic of discussion about the Station, to move forward. By three that afternoon the tickets had been obtained from a businessman, who had planned to attend with his wife, but got called off to Rome on an urgent matter.

With tickets in hand, Quentin popped the question—not the *big* pop, just the date question—and Ann accepted. The destination of their "outing", as he called it, not "date", was top secret. Ann feigned ignorance and curiosity to play along, but had, of course, already been let in on the secret by Tonya. Ann was more than excited, for Elaine Paige's rendition of *Memories* was perhaps her favorite song of all time and absolutely no one could equal it. If ever she were given the choice between being a human and cat, especially a singing dancing cat, the decision was clear: cat! She imagined herself walking along the top of a picket fence, singing, standing beneath a streetlight, singing, perched upon a trashcan in a lonely alley, singing... always singing, though, if the truth be known, singing wasn't exactly her gift. No matter... dreaming was and she would pursue it gladly.

Throughout the next three days Ann danced about, humming and singing the tunes and songs from the Musical. These were indeed some of her favorites. She wondered why they didn't play more of them on the radio but then remembered all the hassle and fuss over royalties, who got them and when. Thankfully, others took care of those details at the Station, for she couldn't stomach it. "Another job I'm glad I don't have," she thought to herself.

They arrived early and had no trouble getting into the Theatre. Before the performance several people introduced themselves, anxious to meet the now famous girl and tiger whose fame was spreading about the City. At last the exits were identified and the audience hushed, as the orchestra took their places and the music began.

Ann wasn't the only fan. One would think that Ravi had also listened to the Musical his whole life, for he swayed back-and-forth with the music and seemed to really get into the characters. Bombalurina resonated with him and if Tavi had been here, the duo may have leapt onto the stage with the singing of *The Rum Tum Tugger*. Ravi definitely felt sorry for Demeter, the troubled and skittish one. Jellylorum's concern for the others was just precious, as was Ravi's reaction to it.

Quentin imagined Ravi with a top hat and cane singing *The Cat About Town* with Bustopher Jones. Ravi sort of snuggled up closer to Ann in reaction to Jemima, the youngest kitty, as she sang *The Moments of Happiness*. Victoria's elegant dancing was definitely a hit with him too.

Somehow Mister Mistoffelees didn't exactly sit right with Ravi. Neither did Old Deuteronomy and Skimbleshanks... perhaps not the right chemistry... definitely not the type to hang out with a very responsible guide and bodyguard worthy of the Secret Service.

Munkustrap, Mungojerrie, and Rumpleteazer were just all wrong— trashcan-raiding alley cats. You could leave them out of the show altogether as far as Ravi was concerned. He let out a little grumble sound to indicate his disapproval—nothing like a roar, of course.

Macavity, Rumpus, and Alonzo had better not show their faces or tails in Ravi's neighborhood unless they want to be tossed in the sewer, where the real rats would eat them for lunch. Someone definitely needs to adjust the script on this one if it's ever going to be a hit with tigers. The rest of the cast was good and performed their parts quite well.

Grizabella... ahh... the magnificent Grizabella... played by the incomparable Elaine Paige. The music... the lights... the voice... the cat of all cats... Grizabella. Ravi was spellbound... enchanted... enthralled... After the last curtain call Quentin leaned in to Ann remarked, "I think Ravi is in love with Elaine Paige."

* * *

They arrived at the Theatre via Grand Central Terminal and entered without trouble regarding Ravi. Perhaps the stories of him had circulated around the City enough that people were getting used to the idea of a Tiger on the Town. The performance was positively glorious, exceeding every expectation. On the way back to the Terminal, Quentin led Ann and Ravi into the Top of the Rock, where they rose to the summit, where many tourists come to take in the spectacular 360-degree skyline view of the City. Even though Ann couldn't see it, somehow the feel of the night air was special.

The three stood and took in the atmosphere in silence, as others milled about, several commenting on Ravi. After nearly a half-hour, Quentin turned to face Ann, then encircled her with his arms and drew her close. Slowly, she turned her face upward. After what seemed hours, their lips met and lingered for several seconds. A pause... Then another kiss... A little longer pause... Followed by a little longer kiss plus a squeeze. At last...

The return trip on the Subway to where Quentin had parked was bliss itself. Ann rode with her head against his chest, which began a little stiff but gradually relaxed so that it felt natural. He pulled her in and squeezed her shoulder. They were *finally* on the way and could honestly consider this a *romantic* relationship.

Chapter 23. The Babies

Quentin should have known these things. He should have put one and one together to get two. He had all the necessary information in a spreadsheet, which did include graphs extrapolated out into the future. Yet somehow it hadn't occurred to him that things were about to happen in the Lab. Three generations of sewer rats were ready to pop plus Izzy, who had been shacking up with Iggy, plus Rocky and Lil, the raccoons from the Tennessee cleanup, were all due to have babies on the same day. Even though the numbers were plain to see, the idea hadn't clicked.

You wouldn't know anything was up from observing the Couch Potatoes, except that half of them were even more distended than the others. The Television Critics were always busy anyway—except, of course, during Wheel of Fortune, which Quentin quickly changed to something else. The Tiny Dancers were twirling and tumbling like they were on meth—half of them, that is. The other half were less than enthusiastic about dancing or even eating. Iggy was a nervous wreck but Izzy was cool as a cucumber. Rocky was clueless—probably his first time being a papa. Lil, who preferred to be called, 'Nancy', was having an emotional meltdown.

Izzy was the first to enter labor, a 'detail' brought to Quentin's attention by a sudden change in Iggy's behavior, which included racing back-and-forth across the keyboard. Before Quentin could save the spreadsheet and close the laptop, two of the sewer rats went into labor. From there the situation exploded into a full-blown episode of Emergency-911 plus General Hospital combined on fast-forward. By nine the next morning there were 24 arrivals: 17 rats, all genetically modified, 4 raccoons, all genetically modified, and 3 iguanas, half genetically modified.

This variety gave them a chance to test the what ifs. The rats were naturally bred but each pair of parents began as modified embryos. Iggy was modified but Izzy wasn't. Neither Rocky nor Lil were modified but their babies were—each with a different tweak of the splicer molecule. Every one of them shared a little part of Quentin. This could get interesting... and scary... more like terrifying.

What if they all did get out?
The sewers would never be the same.
That's not funny.
This is no time to make jokes.

As Quentin struggled to get his mind around this next phase of life in the Lab, another song rose up from the depths of his memory...

Somewhere in the Black Hills of Dakota
There lived a young boy named Rocky Raccoon
Who booked a small room
In the local Saloon
Only to find Gideon's Bible...

For the first time in this long process of genetic experimentation Quentin questioned whether or not it was *ethical* in the big sense. He and Booth had good intentions. They never meant to harm anyone or anything. Still, it was clearly meddling in what many people would consider sacred ground: life itself. Maybe tigers and sewer rats weren't meant to be smart. Perhaps iguanas shouldn't mess with a computer mouse or PowerPoint. Would Rocky and Lil be better off in a Dakota Saloon or their offspring performing at the Grand Ole Opry? The truth is... Quentin had no idea and hadn't given it much thought before now.

* * *

On the following morning, just before the noon radio show, Quentin and Ann sat across the table at the Café. The atmosphere was perfect and the conversation pleasant. She fairly beamed and he was basking in the light. Then the alternate universe swapped with this one...

"So what would you do if I said I was going to have a baby?" Ann asked.

Quentin tried desperately to grasp the edges of the wormhole connecting the two universes and return to the first one. This struggle was interrupted by his cup crashing to the table and a sea of coffee spreading out, engulfing the cosmos.

"But we never..." he stuttered.

"Of course not," she corrected. "Tonya's pregnant, not me. But what will you do when I eventually am pregnant, after we get married, of course?"

"Oh, yes, of course, when we get married," he stammered. "And then we... you know... and you get... like you know... and then have a... you know... like a b... ba..."

"Baby," she finished for him. "It's OK. You can say it. Even though we aren't married. We can still talk about it."

"Yes, of course, talk about 'it' and the other thing and the you know and also the thing that we do before we do the thing or the other thing..."

"It would change a lot of things."

"Yes, definitely, change a lot of things... diapers and like stuff..."

"It would be complicated, working at the Station and nursing a baby."

"You could be a papoose... I mean get a backpack thing... or we could get a saddle for Ravi. I'm sure he'd be OK with that."

90

"It's a little more complicated than transportation," Ann explained. "That's why I thought we should discuss it."

"Oh, yes, complicated... very complicated..." Quentin quickly agreed.

"Babies can be a lot of work, especially with my challenges."

"Yes, tell me about it," Quentin exclaimed. "Babies are popping out everywhere these days and the guys in the Lab are going nuts. We've started watching this YouTube channel that's just for new dads and we're all learning so much. We're in this thing together, of course. Us *guys* gotta support each other, you know."

"I thought it was just you and Booth plus a random person that comes in from time-to-time from another site," Ann puzzled.

"Oh, no, I meant the *guys*," Quentin explained. "Three generations of sewer rats. I guess there are four or six generations now, depending on how you count them, plus the iguanas and the raccoons. Rocky is clueless but Iggy is very supportive."

With this clarification said, Ann spewed her coffee, adding it to the already spreading mess. It would take a roll of paper towel to clean this up.

As they mopped up coffee, Ann continued to laugh. "I'm glad that when I eventually do get pregnant and have a baby you will have such stalwart fellows as Rocky the Raccoon and Iggy the Iguana to help you through the process. I've heard that Lamaze classes can be a challenge too. Maybe Izzy and Lil, or is it, 'Nancy', will be there for me too."

At this moment, Tonya arrived and remarked, "Sorry I'm late. I was looking at some new stretchy pants. I see you've already had coffee. Is there any left or did you two splash it all?"

"We were just talking about babies," Ann explained. "And Quentin was telling me about his emotional support team, which consists of a raccoon and iguana."

"How very interesting," Tonya balked.

"You won't believe it," Quentin said breathlessly. "In the past twenty-four hours we've had twenty-four babies: seventeen rats, four raccoons, and three iguanas. I'm going to have to open a daycare center and probably home school the entire lot. I mean, like what school would take them on? Someone's got to teach them how to get by in a world that will treat them like any other rodent. I know what it's like to be excluded and bullied just for being different. I couldn't bear for them to go through that without a support system firmly in place."

"No, of course not," Tonya chuckled.

"What will it be like when the other rats want to go raid a trashcan and my guys want to play a video game or watch a movie?"

"Oh, the challenges of parenthood," Ann laughed.

91

"Maybe they could start a band," Tonya suggested.

"I mean, they've already got Rocky Raccoon," Ann added.

"That's a great idea!" Quentin exclaimed.

"I was just kidding," Tonya admitted.

"Me too," Ann confessed.

"No, seriously," Quentin said excitedly. "It really is a great idea. The Band would bring them all together in spite of their differing species."

Chapter 24. The Quiz

Quentin had been racking his brain trying to figure out a regular weekly event that would be fun for Ann plus work as a date. Finally, he hit on the idea after talking to one of the random technicians that spent three days in the Laboratory running samples through one of the several analyzers. A pizza joint not too far from a stop on the Subway and on the same Line as the one near the Radio Station had a trivia quiz on Tuesday nights. The winning table didn't have to pay their bill. It ticked several boxes and would be a treat for some time to come.

The first night Quentin and Ann sat at a table by themselves and easily won the contest. After that, another table invited them to join. At this larger table were two couples, one recently married and the other soon-to-be. This too worked out well, as Ann saw it, for when not answering trivia questions, the discussion often drifted to engagement, marriage, and even *babies*. All three topics made Quentin nervous and in increasing order with the topic of babies reaching the level of bone-chilling terror.

As hoped, and not surprisingly, the more these topics were discussed, the less terrified Quentin became—not that he would ever be *comfortable* with such, but at least moving in the right direction. Another plus for this new activity was more diverse conversations; that is, the others talked more and Quentin talked less. They had somewhat *normal* lives, which didn't involve working all day in a laboratory with genetically modified super smart rodents, lizards, and raccoons—or Bengal tigers on a leash either, nor were they blind or nerdy—just normal young people building lives together in the City.

This Mosaic Quiz Team, as they called themselves, consistently won, which pleased them well enough. The two other guys could handle any sports-related question. One of the gals was an encyclopedia of historical trivia and the other could rattle off the cast of any movie, the director, the producer, when it came out, and what awards it had won. Quentin, of course, covered all the science questions, like who invented the lug nut, the steering wheel, and the windshield wiper. Ann occasionally came up with an answer, mostly about novels, the characters, and who wrote them. She had listened to every Agatha Christie book ever turned audible plus every book written by Jane Austin and Stephen King. Quentin noted that a surprising number of book-related questions led back to Jane Austin. When asked the source of the questions, he was told that they came from a website and that the Pizza Shop paid a nominal fee for the subscription—not that just anyone could get these questions.

Many nights, as Ann laughed with the group, answered questions, and ate pizza, she considered the irony of them attending the weekly Quiz, yet Quentin never asking the much more important questions, which would move them along in their relationship and life together. Each day she had to remind herself that this was progress and that eventually they would get around to it. One night several of the questions were about celebrities, who was married to who, and for how long. For example: How many times were Elizabeth Taylor and Richard Burton married and divorced? No response from Quentin that night. On another evening the question actually came up about the average age of marriage and length of engagement, also nothing out of Quentin on the way home.

* * *

And then one night it happened... Perhaps the planets were finally aligned. Perhaps the aliens left Roswell and returned to Mars. Perhaps Iggy or Rocky finally prevailed upon Quentin to make the move. Whatever, it happened...

As they were walking back from the Pizza Shop to the Subway, Quentin spoke... "So, like, Ann, I've been thinking..."

"A dangerous thing, I know," Ann replied with a singsong tone, quoting the line from Gaston in Disney's Beauty and the Beast. She couldn't help it but regretted the words as they came out of her mouth.

"There's something I've been meaning to ask you..."

"Keep your mouth shut, girl. Don't say anything. Just wait for it," she told herself.

"Let's just stop here for a second," he pleaded. She could sense his whole demeanor changing. Perhaps this was *it.*

"Would you ever consider living with me?" he stammered. "Forever, I mean... not like just for the weekend or anything like that. No, I don't mean *living* with, not like that... of course not like *that*... nothing at all like that. I mean like forever and always... I mean marriage. Like the husband and wife kind of thing. You know, with a ring sort of like..."

Ann felt something brush against her hand, which startled her so that she drew back.

"Please... please take it," he begged. "Don't push it away."

"Take what?"

"Oh, it's a ring," he explained. "In a box. You know, like from a jewelry store. Here, feel it..."

She reached out tentatively to touch the open box.

"It's a *real* ring. Honest, I promise... with a *real* diamond from an actual jewelry store. I swear. I would never try to trick you with a plastic one or anything like that."

She held the little box in her hand by this time and pulled the ring out. After feeling it, she slid it on her finger. Surprise didn't begin to describe this feeling. Astonishment was more like it... right on the sidewalk, no less.

"I'm on my knee down here," he added. "Both knees actually. I'm begging... literally begging... *please*..."

Tears began to run down her face as she reached out to touch his.

"I have witnesses, honest! People are watching us."

She touched his face and then felt his head turn.

"Hey, Lady! Speak up. Please tell her that this is for real. I need some support here."

The tears turned to laughter as he extended the call.

"Buddy, please! Come check the ring and help me out here."

The voice of an old man replied, "Well, Sweetheart, Lover Boy is definitely on his knees and the article in question looks to be real from here. It even sparkles in the streetlight. Of course, I ain't comin no closer, what with Tony the Tiger there to possibly have me for supper, but the whole thing looks legit to me."

Seconds passed, yet she knew not what to say.

The old man continued. "So, are you gunna put this guy out of his misery and say, 'yes' or leave him on his knees to suffer?"

Before Ann could reply, Quentin interjected, "I've had it for months now. I just couldn't get up the guts to ask you. I've still got the receipt and everything."

She said, "Rise, yon Prince, for I accept your proposal of marriage!"

As Quentin staggered to his feet, the voice of an old woman cried out with disgust, "This is ridiculous! They're probably making a video for that Ticky Tacky or whatever."

"Kiss me, Prince, before I turn back into a toad or a tiger or whatever," Ann demanded.

Quentin clumsily advanced until he was hugging and kissing her... at last...

Several more people had assembled to watch this unfolding spectacle. Laughter fluttered into the night sky, as one voice said, "This is one for the record books."

"No one will believe this," said another voice.

Their lips parted and she said, "I guess we've entertained these nice people long enough."

As if this whole thing hadn't been surprising enough up until this point, Quentin stepped back, lifted Ann's hand in his, bowed, and proclaimed, "Fairest Princess, I take thee now to yon Subway, which shall suffice, since I have no trusty steed upon which to ride with thee off into the moonset or whatever it may be called in the middle of the night."

The only one who maintained any dignity during this silly spontaneous play upon the sidewalk was Ravi, who sat through the whole thing, wagging his head.

Chapter 25. The Plans

Engaged! With a date to be *married*! Could this possibly be? Was this happening to her? With ever-shy Quentin, no less? Did she ever think they would spend the rest of their lives together when they were tumbling about on the floor with the desk, backpacks, and dog? The sporadic, awkward conversations in the hallway and lunchroom might lead to more? In truth, her life had been an adventure since that knock on the door when he showed up with a "replacement" guide that turned out to be a tiger—no, an adventure from the very beginning. She could hardly imagine her life without Ravi and now without Quentin. There would eventually be babies, but let's not consider those logistics at this time. We'll have to come back to that later... not too much later, as they weren't kids anymore, but they had to actually tie the proverbial knot before that could happen.

He had finally done it. Dropped to his knees on the sidewalk in the City, mere blocks from the Pizza Shop. It had actually happened. She reached out and had taken the little box from his hand, found the ring, and slipped it onto her finger. Of course, she had said, 'yes'. If not, he might have fainted and Ravi may have been compelled performed CPR. There had even been witnesses. Someone had even taken a picture with a phone, which appeared in an obscure section of the paper—not the Times, of course, but the throw away paper that is free but filled with advertisements. The response had been so enthusiastic that the paper called with the promise to do a piece on their wedding and supply a *real* photographer.

* * *

Tonya quickly volunteered to be Maid of Honor and the entire Station Crew were poised to assist in any and every way possible. Renting Carnegie Hall or Madison Square Gardens wasn't necessary, though one of the technicians had suggested these venues. The little Church near her folks place was available and experienced, ready to schedule weddings. Of course, the Reception would be held at 7-7-6. The grandmothers were already planning the menu. The Plans were rolling forward so smoothly she could hardly believe it was happening.

Quentin had undergone a remarkable transition too. He now gently kissed her at every opportunity... when they met for coffee, when he excused himself to go to the bathroom and when he came back, when he picked her up at the Apartment and the Radio Station too. When he dropped her off at her apartment, he applied a proper hug and kiss. The change was truly like a fairy tale come true, which she had hoped for but never planned to living out.

They even talked about living space. Would it work better if he moved in with her or if she moved in with him or if they got a new place? There were several options to consider. Not surprisingly, he showed up one day with the results of a spreadsheet comparing everywhere they might live plus various travel options to the Radio Station and the Laboratory. The ideal location was a condo that wasn't absurdly expensive plus there were some units available. It would work, but it would also mean owning instead of renting and neither were quite sure they wanted to take that step just yet. They finally settled on him moving into her place while they decided. Stuff that didn't fit would be stored at one or the other Parent's houses.

At some point during this conversation the topic of a room for the baby or babies came up, which would change the requirements and condo options. Surprisingly, Quentin did not go into cardiac arrest or even seem in much of a panic. She could well remember how he reacted to this subject in the past and so, yes, they had come a long way already and it was good. It was hard to believe this was the same awkward guy she had sat on in high school.

Quentin even talked more about them and their life together than about the latest development in the Lab, though he did provide periodic updates on the twenty-four kiddos, some of which exceeded their expectations, while others failed to exhibit any remarkable abilities. That success in such an incredibly complicated process was not likely to come easily or continuously was becoming obvious, even to Quentin, though Booth had been more cautiously optimistic from the outset.

Either Iggy the Iguana or Randy the Raccoon, the most remarkable of the four offspring, accompanied Quentin to the Café and on their dates. Strange animals on public transportation had almost become the norm by this time. Randy was always there on Quiz night and they all joked that he knew the answers before anyone else. People were always calling for him to perform something, perhaps sing any one of the Beatles' hits or play a musical instrument. Better still... quote from Gideon's Bible. Not surprisingly, he could do none of these things, but he could win the shell game and even pick a winning blackjack hand. Strange that most people just thought these to be well-trained pets. Few brought up the subject of genetic meddling or the potential risks that were surely inevitable. After all, has there *ever* been a SiFi movie made in which such was tried and turned out *good* in the end? Didn't all of these stories end with someone—if not the star, of course—being chased and eaten?

Booth was more concerned with these matters than was Quentin. Teaching, feeding, and playing with the laboratory kiddos was consuming more and more of Quentin's time so that there wasn't much new being added to the research database. That didn't mean there was any less budget spent. In fact, the budget continued to creep upward. In the past few weeks and months, Booth had been involved in more cleanup operations in other locations, some over seas and was spending more time traveling and less in the Laboratory.

98

The original four Mousebusters had been deployed twice more, not at NIMH to recover mice but first at a military base to locate missing wristbands containing vital security codes, which must not fall into the wrong hands. The second time was to Guantanamo Bay, where they were part of an elaborate ruse to trick three terrorists into revealing their plans to create mayhem. They knew they'd been had when four rats performed a choreographed dance number just outside their cell, just beyond reach, just like their chances.

* * *

Ann's promotion and raise came through at the Radio Station sooner than expected and this expanded their options. Tonya was out on maternity leave by this time and another woman had moved from a night spot to the afternoon with Ann so that the team of four—two DJs plus two technicians—was maintained. An intern who had been hoping for a position took the open night spot and promised to step back or whatever if Tonya returned and wanted her position again. Life for Ann and Quentin was starting to look a little more like the rest of the world and that was a good thing.

President Bates' second term had ended and the family returned to Vermont. Darcy was glad to leave DC and the fuss of the big city. Some of the Secret Service agents were reassigned to Vermont but not 3M. Milton, Marks, and Mearns were still on the night shift but the new President's children were all grown and living elsewhere. They missed Darcy and Tavi and their adventures together. It would be quite boring from here on out. Darcy insisted on attending the wedding and was promptly made a bride's maid. Of course Ravi and Tavi would be there too as ring bearers.

* * *

Booth put down the phone and looked blankly into the distance thinking. Quentin noticed the silence, then the expression, and wondered. A smile began to form on Booth's face.

"So..." Quentin prodded.

"You know... There's always someone lost at sea and the Navy could use help from time-to-time. It's not just the other branches of the Military with challenges these days."

"And..."

"It seems that a Biologist at Sea World knows a Commander at the Naval Ship Yard in San Diego who knows a Captain at the Pentagon who is in a Pilates Class with our Colonel, who's always got the General's ear."

"And..."

"Have you ever been to Sea World?"

"No, but I'm sure it would be fun. Exactly where is this leading?"

99

"I wonder how big a blue whale embryo is... when it's just one cell, of course?"

"I'm game," Quentin chimed in. "As long as we don't name it Willie because this one will get out."

The Characters

Auro: golden retriever and literal *tiger mom*

barganelle (bar-ga-nelle): the donor organism

Bates, Darcy: blind daughter of POTUS

Booth, Dr. Peter: lecturer with connections

bromotrifluorobenzene (bromo-tri-fluoro-benzene): the game changer

Croft, Professor: vowed to destroy Quentin

cyclodeclamide (cyclo-dec-la-mide): the splicer molecule

Draper, Ann: the girl, DJ at WNYG-FM in NYC

Draper, Dennis: Ann's Dad

Draper, Margaret: Ann's Mom

Farley, Jamie: Quentin's Mom

Farley, Quentin: the awkward guy

Farley, William (Bill): Quentin's Dad

Franklin, Tonya: co-worker

Harper, Beth: Deputy Director of Homeland Security

Kirk, Dr.: NIMH

Marks, George: Secret Service Agent

Mearns, Meghan: Secret Service Agent

Milton, Robert: Secret Service Agent

muceladidae (mu-cela-did-ae): the recipient organism

NIMH: National Institute of Mental Health

Percy Air Force Base: where the molecules came together

Price, Dr.: NIMH

procilenna (pro-ci-len-na): didn't work out

Ravi Tiger, Sgt. USMC: the ultimate guard

Scooby: Darcy's guide dog, who is old and near retirement

Tavi: Ravi's twin brother

Toby: the guide dog—protector and friend

Vance, Chuck: the outdoorsy brother-in-law

Vance, Stephanie: Peter's sister

also by D. James Benton

3D Articulation: Using OpenGL, ISBN-9798596362480, Amazon, 2021 (book 3 in the 3D series).

3D Models in Motion Using OpenGL, ISBN-9798652987701, Amazon, 2020 (book 2 in the 3D series.

3D Rendering in Windows: How to display three-dimensional objects in Windows with and without OpenGL, ISBN-9781520339610, Amazon, 2016 (book 1 in the 3D series).

A Synergy of Short Stories: The whole may be greater than the sum of the parts, ISBN-9781520340319, Amazon, 2016.

Azeotropes: Behavior and Application, ISBN-9798609748997, Amazon, 2020.

bat-Elohim: Book 3 in the Little Star Trilogy, ISBN-9781686148682, Amazon, 2019.

Boilers: Performance and Testing, ISBN: 9798789062517, Amazon 2021.

Combined 3D Rendering Series: 3D Rendering in Windows®, 3D Models in Motion, and 3D Articulation, ISBN-9798484417032, Amazon, 2021.

Complex Variables: Practical Applications, ISBN-9781794250437, Amazon, 2019.

Compression & Encryption: Algorithms & Software, ISBN-9781081008826, Amazon, 2019.

Computational Fluid Dynamics: an Overview of Methods, ISBN-9781672393775, Amazon, 2019.

Computer Simulation of Power Systems: Programming Strategies and Practical Examples, ISBN-9781696218184, Amazon, 2019.

Contaminant Transport: A Numerical Approach, ISBN-9798461733216, Amazon, 2021.

CPUnleashed! Tapping Processor Speed, ISBN-9798421420361, Amazon, 2022.

Curve-Fitting: The Science and Art of Approximation, ISBN-9781520339542, Amazon, 2016.

Death by Tie: It was the best of ties. It was the worst of ties. It's what got him killed., ISBN-9798398745931, Amazon, 2023.

Differential Equations: Numerical Methods for Solving, ISBN-9781983004162, Amazon, 2018.

Equations of State: A Graphical Comparison, ISBN-9798843139520, Amazon, 2022.

Evaporative Cooling: The Science of Beating the Heat, ISBN-9781520913346, Amazon, 2017.

Forecasting: Extrapolation and Projection, ISBN-9798394019494, Amazon 2023.

Heat Engines: Thermodynamics, Cycles, & Performance Curves, ISBN-9798486886836, Amazon, 2021.

Heat Exchangers: Performance Prediction & Evaluation, ISBN-9781973589327, Amazon, 2017.

Heat Recovery Steam Generators: Thermal Design and Testing, ISBN-9781691029365, Amazon, 2019.

Heat Transfer: Heat Exchangers, Heat Recovery Steam Generators, & Cooling Towers, ISBN-9798487417831, Amazon, 2021.

Heat Transfer Examples: Practical Problems Solved, ISBN-9798390610763, Amazon, 2023.

The Kick-Start Murders: Visualize revenge, ISBN-9798759083375, Amazon, 2021.

Jamie2: Innocence is easily lost and cannot be restored, ISBN-9781520339375, Amazon, 2016-18.

Kyle Cooper Mysteries: Kick Start, Monte Carlo, and Waterfront Murders, ISBN-9798829365943, Amazon, 2022.

The Last Seraph: Sequel to Little Star, ISBN-9781726802253, Amazon, 2018.

Little Star: God doesn't do things the way we expect Him to. He's better than that! ISBN-9781520338903, Amazon, 2015-17.

Living Math: Seeing mathematics in every day life (and appreciating it more too), ISBN-9781520336992, Amazon, 2016.

Logic+Reason=>Truth: Thinking in the Age of Feeling, ISBN-9798333235022, Amazon 2024.

Lost Cause: If only history could be changed..., ISBN-9781521173770, Amazon, 2017.

Mass Transfer: Diffusion & Convection, ISBN-9798702403106, Amazon, 2021.

Mill Town Destiny: The Hand of Providence brought them together to rescue the mill, the town, and each other, ISBN-9781520864679, Amazon, 2017.

Monte Carlo Murders: Who Killed Who and Why, ISBN-9798829341848, Amazon, 2022.

Monte Carlo Simulation: The Art of Random Process Characterization, ISBN-9781980577874, Amazon, 2018.

Nonlinear Equations: Numerical Methods for Solving, ISBN-9781717767318, Amazon, 2018.

Numerical Calculus: Differentiation and Integration, ISBN-9781980680901, Amazon, 2018.

Numerical Methods: Nonlinear Equations, Numerical Calculus, & Differential Equations, ISBN-9798486246845, Amazon, 2021.

Orthogonal Functions: The Many Uses of, ISBN-9781719876162, Amazon, 2018.

Overwhelming Evidence: A Pilgrimage, ISBN-9798515642211, Amazon, 2021.

Particle Tracking: Computational Strategies and Diverse Examples, ISBN-9781692512651, Amazon, 2019.

Plumes: Delineation & Transport, ISBN-9781702292771, Amazon, 2019.

Power Plant Performance Curves: for Testing and Dispatch, ISBN-9798640192698, Amazon, 2020.

Practical Linear Algebra: Principles & Software, ISBN-9798860910584, Amazon, 2023.

Props, Fans, & Pumps: Design & Performance, ISBN-9798645391195, Amazon, 2020.

Remediation: Contaminant Transport, Particle Tracking, & Plumes, ISBN-9798485651190, Amazon, 2021.

ROFL: Rolling on the Floor Laughing, ISBN-9781973300007, Amazon, 2017.

Seminole Rain: You don't choose destiny. It chooses you, ISBN-9798668502196, Amazon, 2020.

Septillionth: 1 in 10^{24}, ISBN-9798410762472, Amazon, 2022.

Software Development: Targeted Applications, ISBN-9798850653989, Amazon, 2023.

Software Recipes: Proven Tools, ISBN-9798815229556, Amazon, 2022.

Steam 2020: to 150 GPa and 6000 K, ISBN-9798634643830, Amazon, 2020.

Thermochemical Reactions: Numerical Solutions, ISBN-9781073417872, Amazon, 2019.

Thermodynamic and Transport Properties of Fluids, ISBN-9781092120845, Amazon, 2019.

Thermodynamic Cycles: Effective Modeling Strategies for Software Development, ISBN-9781070934372, Amazon, 2019.

Thermodynamics - Theory & Practice: The science of energy and power, ISBN-9781520339795, Amazon, 2016.

Version-Independent Programming: Code Development Guidelines for the Windows® Operating System, ISBN-9781520339146, Amazon, 2016.

The Waterfront Murders: As you sow, so shall you reap, ISBN-9798611314500, Amazon, 2020.

Weather Data: Where To Get It and How To Process It, ISBN-9798868037894, Amazon, 2023.

Made in the USA
Monee, IL
23 December 2024

72056635R00066